BOUGHT BY THE SHEIKH

DIANA FRASER

PROLOGUE

"*I* can't go to Gharb Havilah," Gabrielle Taylor repeated, this time with more emphasis. "I simply cannot go." She cleared her throat and sat up straighter, eyeing her professor directly, willing her to accept her refusal without explanation. But one look at her narrowing gaze, and she knew it wasn't going to be so easy.

Not for the first time, Gabrielle wished that her head of department was a stereotypical Oxford University professor —absent-minded and with a less than firm grip on the college's finances. Instead, it had been her luck to have someone intent on turning her Oxford college into a profitable institution.

"Gabrielle, I'll do you the courtesy of speaking plainly. If you *don't* take this consultancy at Gharb Havilah, if you *don't* go to the palace and do what's required, you will no longer have a place at this college. In fact, not only will *you* not have a place, nor will precisely four of your colleagues. We cannot afford to keep our present number of staff without this funding. Very *generous* funding, I might add."

Gabrielle swallowed, trying to moisten her suddenly dry

mouth. "There must be some mistake." As her professor leaned forward across the desk, she realized it was her who'd made the mistake.

"No mistake, Gabrielle. The college has been running on empty for years, supported by the coffers of other more prosperous colleges. We *need* this grant, and you *will* get it for us."

She nodded, realizing she'd been cornered. She had nowhere else to turn. This college had been her home, her savior, her whole life, since well, she never thought of what went before—it was still too painful. And to return to that? She leaned forward, gesturing impotently. "But you don't understand."

The professor shook her head impatiently. "You're right, I don't. You've told me nothing that would suggest a return trip to Gharb Havilah wouldn't be appropriate, no, wouldn't be *ideal* at this point in your career. You lived there for the first eighteen years of your life and on and off since. You know its culture, its artifacts first hand, as well as the people." She sat back in her chair and threw her hands in the air. "Come on, Gabrielle, what could prevent you from returning there?"

She should tell her. *Now*. She sucked in stuffy, over-heated air, and tried to grasp at reasons, at words, but only one thing entered her mind and refused to leave—the image of a man, a man who she'd loved so much that she'd walked away from him. She looked up into the gray eyes of this Oxford don and knew that there was no point in telling her. There was no way that those eyes would be swayed by love. But, apparently, although she couldn't convey the truth, she'd managed to convey her resignation to her professor.

"Good. Then we won't hear any more about the matter. Make your travel arrangements with my secretary, sort out your personal life, and be in Gharb Havilah in one month."

"A month? Is that all the notice I get?"

"And how much do you need?" The professor's sarcastic tone was barely concealed. "Your rooms at the college will still be here when you return. You have no pets, no dependents. Maybe you have a man, or woman, to whom you're close?"

Gabrielle shook her head vehemently. She'd made sure she had no ties, especially of the heart. Because you couldn't love someone if your heart was broken. It was as if the edges of her heart had cracked and sealed over, never to heal— cooled by her academic work, cauterized by her loneliness.

"Good. Then that's settled. You'll fulfill the requirements of the contract to the letter."

"But I'm an archaeologist. What do *I* know about public relations?"

"They obviously believe you know something." The professor scrolled through the contract on her laptop. "Here it is. They want *stories*, apparently. Stories around the artifacts about which you are the foremost expert." She crossed her arms and turned her steely gaze upon Gabrielle once more.

"Stories?"

"Stories. Make them up if you have to, but fulfill this contract because otherwise there won't be a job for you to return to."

"And it's for only a month?"

"One month. The contract ends on the day of the country's bi-millennial celebration. I'm sure you'll be able to make up stories for one month?" She snapped her laptop shut—a cue for Gabrielle to leave. "There's money at stake, and there's the future of the college at stake. It depends on you. Don't let me down."

Gabrielle's mouth was dry with fear as she left the office. It wasn't until she was the other side of the office door that the full force of her repressed emotions washed over her. She leaned back against the closed door, suddenly feeling faint.

"Are you okay?" the professor's secretary asked. "You look as if you've seen a ghost."

Gabrielle nodded. "Yes," she replied ambiguously. She walked past the secretary, who was apparently reassured that Gabrielle was okay. But Gabrielle was far from okay, because she'd been confronted with a ghost—a ghost from her past, a ghost she'd hoped she'd never see again, a ghost she'd had no choice but to leave twelve months earlier.

CHAPTER 1

King Zavian bin Ameen Al Rasheed checked the clock, picked up another report from the pile, and continued to dictate to his secretary. But his mind refused to focus completely on his paperwork. A part of it drifted to the image of a woman—long blonde hair, and eyes that could wound at a thousand feet. But now, instead of imagining her amid the spires and steeples of Oxford, wondering what she was doing, he knew what she was doing. She would be putting away her laptop—he knew there was no way Gabrielle would miss working on an uninterrupted twelve-hour flight—and doing up her seat belt as the plane prepared for its final descent into Gharb Havilah.

He fell silent and turned his head to look out the window, up into the white-hot sky of a June morning, and imagined he could see her plane. And her on it, her eyes moving to the window, seeking out her first glimpse of Gharb Havilah after twelve long months.

"Your Majesty?"

He turned back to his secretary. "Yes?"

"Did you wish to complete your response to this report?"

He looked down at the papers and tried to refocus. He had no idea where he was, which was exactly why he needed Gabrielle in Gharb Havilah.

His secretary prompted him with the last words he'd dictated, enabling him to continue. When he'd finished, he gestured with his hand. "You may go." As soon as his secretary had left, his gaze returned to the clock, and his vizier quietly entered the room.

"Ah, Naseer, it's time, then."

The vizier's hooded eyes narrowed with disapproval. Zavian knew his vizier's thoughts on his plans, but, for once, wasn't prepared to discuss them. They were nonnegotiable. There was no way he could continue with half his mind on Gabrielle and half on running his kingdom. No, he wanted her here, and he wanted her out of his system. The reality of being with her must surely reduce his need for her, bring it back into proportion. Because if there was one thing he'd learned from his vizier, it was that familiarity bred contempt. But he didn't require contempt. He needed only to slacken his obsession, and slake his thirst, so he didn't need her anymore.

Zavian walked toward the door, but before he could leave, Naseer coughed. Zavian swallowed back his impatience. He respected Naseer. He'd been his father's advisor and got the job done, and done well. But one thing he wished his vizier wasn't, was so subtle. It made him impatient. "What is it, Naseer?" He tapped his fingers against the door handle, wanting to get going, to see the person who'd consumed his every waking and sleeping moment for the past twelve months.

"She isn't on the flight."

Zavian ground his teeth. He'd been precise about the contract. Nothing had been left to chance, let alone the travel arrangements. "Get that professor on the phone and demand to know why."

Again the deceptively obsequious bow of the head—his vizier was anything but submissive. "There is no need for that."

"Why?"

"Because I have tracked her movements. She's traveled overland. She's still arriving today, but by a different entry point."

Zavian drew in a jagged breath. He'd done everything to bring her to him, and she was close now, and yet she still managed to change his plans without his knowledge. Nothing had changed. Catching Gabrielle was like trying to hold water in the palm of your hand, like trying to contain starlight on an oasis. You think you have it for a few satisfactory moments only to find that it's left you, following a course of its own devising, leaving you all the more obsessed with retrieving it again.

"She cashed in her first-class ticket and is journeying through neighboring countries and entering through the desert border control. No doubt reminiscing about growing up with her ridiculous grandfather."

Zavian decided to overlook his vizier's slur on Gabrielle's grandfather—the result of an old feud that went back far beyond Zavian's time. Zavian had always liked Gabrielle's grandfather. More than liked—he'd been there for Zavian when his own family hadn't. "Take me there."

"What is the point? She'll be arriving at the palace later today as arranged."

"The point is, Naseer, that I wish to see her arrive. I wish to see her walk into my country with my own eyes. I need to know she's here."

His vizier shook his head. "I hope you know what you're doing."

7

"Of course. As you, yourself, have said, obsessions result from a lack. I intend to make sure I have no lack, and then the obsession will ease."

"It may not ease completely."

"It doesn't need to. Anything less than an obsession I can deal with, anything less than an obsession can be buried deep."

Naseer nodded, his mouth twisting as he resisted vocalizing his doubts, which Zavian could read in his eyes. "I have a car waiting."

As Zavian strode through the old palace, along the secret corridors constructed by his great grandfather for security, his thoughts were still of Gabrielle. He knew what she was doing. He'd made sure she had to come, and she was trying to arrive incognito, trying to resist his command. She surely couldn't have forgotten what life was like here. How he controlled everything, just as his father had done before him, and his before him. She'd always thought she was better than him, that she could outwit him. She was an innocent still. An innocent with whom he was obsessed. But not for much longer.

It was a half-hour winding drive to the border crossing, up through the narrow mountain range which divided the high desert from the plain upon which the city lay. A cluster of palm trees indicated the site of what was once a small village centered around a well. The village was long gone, cleared by his unscrupulous great grandfather, replaced by utilitarian buildings for the border guards.

"Stop here." They parked some distance from the other cars—one, a taxi, the others no doubt belonging to the border control officers—and watched from the shade of the palm grove. He glanced at his driver, who'd pressed his earpiece closer to his ear.

"Five minutes," said the driver, knowing what his king required—accurate information at all times.

Zavian stepped out of the car and stood under the tree beside the oasis, filled after the recent rains. He looked out to the quiet, sun-bleached desert where nothing moved. Immediately in front of him was his own border control hut. Shimmering in the distance he could see the hut of the border control belonging to the neighboring country, Tawazun, with whom the three countries which comprised the ancient lands of Havilah hoped to unite through marriage. But Zavian had no thoughts of the Tawazun princess, with whom his marriage was being brokered at this very moment.

Between Tawazun's border and his own was an empty no-man's-land, broken only by the barest of tracks. This was a place where Bedouin had lived for centuries, their movements ebbing and flowing with the seasons. Trust the arrogant Gabrielle to imagine she could use the route undetected. No, Zavian reflected. Not arrogant. Gabrielle was many things, but she wasn't arrogant. Her decision was more likely a result of a naive sentimentality.

A radio crackled with the jarring guitar riff of an American pop song, its electronic whine incongruous in the setting. His eyes watered as he concentrated on the white light of the far checkpoint. His eyes narrowed as he found what he was looking for—a swirl of sand that filled the bright blue sky and sent a jolt through his body. He sucked in the hot, dry air to calm his response to the merest suggestion of her presence.

She emerged from the shadows of the lone building to walk the five-hundred-yard stretch through no-man's-land, the details of her form slowly becoming visible beneath the moving cloud of sand. She was wearing a full-length gray abaya with a long scarf around her head, which the desert breeze lifted until it became one with the cloud of sand which punctuated each step. Finally, she stopped to speak to border control, her hand pressed to her chest, trying to keep her scarf in place while presenting her passport documents.

She could have been anyone. Large sunglasses covered her eyes, and her robes were cheap, the sort a common Bedouin woman in the market might have worn. She wanted to pass unnoticed. She'd failed. There was nothing about her movements, or figure, that would ever allow her to pass unnoticed, not to his eyes anyway. She had a grace, a swaying feminine gait, which was entirely her own, altogether seductive, even if she was completely unaware of it. It was natural, he knew that much. Undesigned. And he felt it all the more keenly because of it.

The land through which she'd just walked was stony and barren—a fitting entry—belonging not to one nation or another, displaced, just like she'd always been. He turned his back on her and returned to the car. He nodded to his driver, and the car purred into motion, leaving behind the lone woman as she re-entered his country. He glanced into the wing mirror and saw a long strand of blonde hair fly out of her abaya, teased by the wind, as she turned at the sound of his car leaving. He remembered the texture of her hair, like silk. He rubbed his fingers together as if reliving the feel of it between his fingertips. He swallowed and looked away.

GABRIELLE WAS BEGINNING to regret her impulsive desire to enter Gharb Havilah from the desert. Somehow she'd forgotten the intensity of the heat. Even the short walk between countries, through no-man's-land, had been challenging, the heat scorching her throat, the wind drying her eyes. She'd forgotten how inhospitable the desert was, how alien, how unforgiving to the people who made their home there. But more than that, she'd forgotten how much she loved it—not in an intellectual way, but at a deep visceral level which clawed at her gut. Its beauty wasn't picture postcard perfect but as raw and uncompromising as its ruler.

She grabbed her scarf and swept it around her face, as she walked the last few yards across the stony, barren land to the Gharb Havilah checkpoint. Both guards were outside watching her approach, which alone indicated how infrequently the border crossing was used. She wasn't even entirely sure why she'd decided to come overland through the mountains where there was no internet. A desire to be incognito, perhaps? Maybe. But also an instinctive need to take things slowly, to re-acquaint herself with the country a little at a time, to let it seep into her being. Far better this than to be offloaded into Gharb Havilah's modern airport where she'd have trouble adjusting from her English world to the country in which she'd been raised.

It had taken a week of travel through the desert she'd used to know so well to get here—a week of attuning herself to its slow pace, and its timeless glamor which she loved so much. Her ability to speak the native tongues, and her old friendships in Tawazun—a country which she knew almost as well as Havilah—ensured her safety.

Yes, she wanted the time to sink herself back into this world again. But she had to admit she also wanted to send a signal—to Zavian. He might call, and she might have to come, but she'd do it her way, on her terms. She was not, and would never be, controlled by him.

But, as she handed over her papers to the guards, her eyes were drawn beyond them, to an expensive-looking car, not a taxi, disappearing into a hazy mirage. It seemed she wasn't the only person seeking entry through that remote spot.

She exchanged pleasantries with the guards as they completed the paperwork. Their responses became friendlier as she answered in their native tongue. But, as she walked toward her taxi, her eyes were once again drawn to the shimmer of the departing car. She suddenly remembered that the border guard had commented on her being the first person that day to cross the border, which meant someone had arrived and then turned back. Why?

She greeted the taxi driver, and he took her battered backpack and placed it in the boot of the car, and they were off, following the faint trace of the previous car toward the capital city of Gharb Havilah. While the driver talked of the country's gossip—the royal family, the state of the economy, and other things of which taxi drivers the world over were experts, Gabrielle's thoughts were entirely on the car she'd seen leaving the border and the registration plate she'd caught a glimpse of. It had to have been him. How on earth had he discovered her changed itinerary? She'd underestimated him, certainly underestimated his compulsion to control everything.

As they emerged from the mountain pass, the city revealed itself, spread across the narrow plain between the mountains and the brilliant blue of the sea. Her heart stopped, held tight by its beauty. The color of terra cotta, the ancient city sat unaltered thanks to centuries of control by the Al Rasheed clan. No high-rise glass buildings for them. It made the world believe they weren't wealthy. The world was wrong. The Al Rasheeds kept their incredible wealth tight, and that knowledge even tighter. They kept their people comfortable and employed, and a tight control upon everything. But it seemed, if the taxi driver's chatter was anything to believe, that things were about to change—that the new sheikh had different ideas. She didn't doubt it.

After the wide-open plains of the high desert, the ancient narrow streets of the old quarter—clogged with cars and people, jostling and shouting as they came closer to the bazaar—was noisy and overwhelming. The taxi turned away from the bazaar and headed toward the palace. Gabrielle leaned forward. "The museum. We need to go to the museum."

"We are, madam."

"But it's back there." She gestured toward the old building, which was soon out of sight, lost amid a jumble of rooftops.

"The museum's administrative center has recently been moved. You wanted to see the person in charge?"

"Yes."

"Then, you will find him at the palace."

Gabrielle felt uneasy as the taxi drove up the wide boulevard—a product of the old King's fascination with all things French—at the end of which stood a medieval castle, situated on a long, low hill which overlooked the city and the sea.

"Please stop here. I'll walk the rest of the way."

The taxi driver shrugged and parked abruptly, blocking off a car trying to emerge from a narrow alleyway. The other vehicle beeped his horn continuously. Her taxi driver yelled expletives while extracting her bag from the boot. She paid him, and he wished her well and drove off, leaving her to walk into the square, busy with tourists and street hawkers. She stepped forward, wanting to be a part of them, needing the anonymity they gave her.

Above the clamor of street traders, tourists and people trying to go about their everyday business, sat the palace—a dominant, aloof presence. Exactly like the new King had become, according to gossip. It was strange to think that the man she knew could have changed so much. She hoped he continued to remain untouchable and aloof because she wanted nothing to do with him.

She had no idea if he was behind her visit or even knew about it. But the strange car at border control nagged at her mind. Who was it? Was it Zavian? But how could it be? He had more to do than track her movements. No, there was absolutely no reason why she and King Zavian bin Ameen Al Rasheed's paths should cross. The palace was vast, and while she'd be working on the PR around the artifacts being exhibited, he'd be ruling the country. She had no wish to stir up anything from the past. There were good reasons why she left—reasons that were still valid, and would always be valid. Zavian was out of her reach, and she intended to keep him that way.

She hitched her backpack higher on her shoulder and approached the palace guard, her papers in hand, prepared for the usual third degree. But, after only a few words, the gate opened without her having to show her documents. Maybe the palace was more accessible than it used to be. Maybe security was lax in keeping with the approach of the new king. Maybe not, she thought as she saw others have their papers scrutinized before being allowed inside the hallowed gardens of the Abyad Palace. She'd barely set foot inside the shady cool of the palace foyer when an official approached her.

"Dr. Taylor. Welcome to the palace. Please, follow me, and I'll take you to your rooms."

Her bag was taken from her, and, unnervingly, they were followed by two more assistants as they walked up the main stairs and turned left. She hesitated. "Excuse me!" she called to the assistant.

"Yes?

"The museum and administrative quarters, surely they'd be in the east wing, with the other public offices and visitor apartments?" He'd made a mistake. He must have been new there.

"Yes, indeed," the young man smiled. "The east wing."

"Then…" she continued, "why are we going to the west?"

The young man assumed a patient smile. "Because I am taking you to your rooms. And they are this way."

Gabrielle's heart sank with a sickening thud. What was going on? She knew full well the implications of staying in the west wing of the palace. That was where the royal family stayed, and only the highest-ranking advisors and relatives. She gripped the staircase, its gold scrollwork digging into her flesh. "No, I'm sorry, but that's not possible."

"Yes, I assure you, it *is* possible, madam. Your suite awaits you."

"No. I'm sorry, I can't stay here. I'll take a room at a hotel." She fumbled for her phone.

"And why would you do that?" His smile appeared stuck fast. "You will be working at the palace, and living at the palace."

"No, really. That's not possible."

"And I say it is." The smile had frozen on his lips. "I apologize, madam, but I have my orders."

She glanced at the two men behind her. They weren't smiling. She looked back at the smiling one as the better of two evils. "Do I have a choice?" She suddenly realized she'd stepped right into a trap.

The smile never wavered. "No, madam."

As she was taken along the grand corridors, past the glimpses of beautiful gardens, she felt as if she were walking in a coiling spiral, taking her ever closer to the heart of the trap.

She was shown to her suite of rooms, and she sat on the large, white silk counterpane and put her head in her hands. What had she done?

GABRIELLE HAD CONSIDERED REFUSING the invitation—more like a command—to attend a reception that evening. But, she had decided there was little point in putting off the moment when she came face to face with the man she'd deserted twelve months earlier. Because now there was no doubt in her mind that it was he who was behind her contract, that it was he who'd made sure she couldn't escape once she'd set foot inside the palace.

A year ago, he'd been the overlooked younger son of the king. Now he *was* king. Something he'd never have been if she'd stayed—something the country needed because, without him, there would have been a civil war. And she couldn't live with that. She'd done the right thing, she said for the millionth time as she walked across the marble hall to the reception room. But the pounding of her heart, the fluttering in her stomach, and the trembling in her hands contradicted her.

She paused briefly on the threshold, struck by a wall of sound—amplified by the marble interior—and a brilliance of light. The sparkle from the crystal chandeliers glanced off the expensive sheen of the ladies' evening dresses and flashed in their diamond jewelry. The overwhelming combination did nothing for her nerves.

She took a glass of sparkling juice from a passing waiter and stood to one side. She hoped she could remain there, unnoticed, until she could safely slip away, her duty having been done. But she had no such luck and was soon immersed in a conversation with the museum director. Suddenly everyone stopped talking, and she knew the king and his entourage must have entered the room. Her heart beat a quick tattoo.

He hadn't changed at all. He was taller than most of them, and she could see him clearly as he scanned the room. The scanning stopped when he saw her. He then said something to the person he was with, and they began to move towards her. She stepped back, but her heels banged against the wall.

To one side, the museum director blocked her way. To the other side, a group of diplomats shifted excitedly at the thought of meeting the king.

His progress was halted from time to time as he was introduced to someone. Then he'd look up and catch her gaze briefly before looking away, his expression registering no recognition, as if he was unaware of her identity. But he was, she knew he was, because each step brought him inexorably closer to her.

And then he reached her. He stood directly in front of her while his assistant introduced them. He held her gaze and, despite her best plans, she couldn't look away.

"And this is Dr. Gabrielle Taylor."

She swallowed and then panicked. How should she greet him? She dropped into the formal curtsey she'd seen the other women offer, but before she could hold it for the required time, he took her hand, and she nearly stumbled from shock. He tightened his grip, giving her the support she needed to raise herself, but derailing her senses in the process. Even when she was standing tall once more, he didn't release his hold.

She could smell his aftershave and a masculinity that sent her legs weak. Close to, she could see her initial impression was wrong. He *had* changed. His mouth, which had been so potent in its capacity to provide pleasure, was firm, grim even, and his gaze was no more promising. But the biggest change was in his eyes. Before, the arrogance had always been there, but it had been tempered by humor and kindness. But she saw nothing of these things in the man before her. No, her overriding impression of him now was power—power to give, and power to take away. She wondered which of those two things he was going to do now, here, with her.

"Dr. Taylor is from Oxford University, here to—"

"I know who she is and why she's here. Welcome, Gabrielle."

She nodded, and smiled nervously, giving a tentative tug on her hand. It didn't yield. "Thank you. It's good to be back." The words tumbled out before she could stop them, because they were true. Gharb Havilah was home to her in a way England would never be. And, as for Zavian... Despite what she insisted to herself she wanted, her body was responding in quite a different way.

His eyes narrowed slightly as he inclined his head toward her in a way that felt intensely intimate. "Is that so?"

"It is..." Her voice faded as she caught the smell of his aftershave. *That* hadn't changed, and it shortcut her defenses, sending a ripple of recognition and desire deep inside her.

He knew. He had to know because he inclined his head further to her, until all she would have to do was stretch up on her tiptoes to feel the caress of his lips against hers.

She cleared her throat. "It is truly good to be back." There was no point denying it.

"Then you should have returned sooner." His thumb swept over the back of her hand, sending pulses of electricity through her body, bringing it to life. She didn't want to be brought to life.

"I was... busy." She summoned up her courage, refusing to allow him to take control of her. He had to know. "And there was no point. Nothing's changed."

His grip lessened on her hand. "Interesting." The chill tone in which the single word was delivered refuted her statement.

"Interesting?" she repeated.

"Yes, I have a feeling I'll find the stories you've been contracted to provide for our prized exhibition pieces, very... illuminating. It's always interesting to know the background of a piece, where it came from, and how it came to be here. Especially the Khasham Qur'an."

She pressed her trembling lips together in an attempt to hold back her feelings and thoughts, which threatened to tumble out chaotically as she suddenly realized why she'd been brought here. He wanted to know how the sixth-century illuminated Qur'an from the ancient city of Khasham had come into his possession.

"The Khasham Qur'an," she repeated huskily, weighing its meaning on her tongue.

"Yes, a subject dear to your heart, I believe. Maybe the only one."

The barb found its target, but she couldn't respond because he'd always known if she'd tried to lie, which left silence the only option.

"And once you've uncovered the story behind its repatriation, then, Dr. Taylor"—he continued—"you may find you have to re-think your assertion that nothing has changed." He dropped her hand. "Enjoy the evening."

He nodded coolly and walked past her before she could respond. Not that she could. It felt like all the air had been sucked out of that warm, crowded reception room, making it difficult to breathe, let alone think. But she could feel. And she wished she couldn't.

He hated her. And she hadn't realized how this knowledge could destroy her. She looked around for an escape, unaware of people talking to her, needing to get away.

ZAVIAN LEFT THE ROOM IMMEDIATELY. He'd organized the reception with only one purpose in mind, and now he'd seen and spoken with her he had no further interest in it. He dismissed his attendants and watched her from behind the one-way mirror. She hadn't changed at all. He suddenly realized that he'd hoped she had. But she hadn't. She shimmered in the traditional abaya—understated and elegant—eclipsing all others as the moon banished the sun, casting a heart-stopping glow over the desert, creating magic where none before existed. Even now, while she twisted and turned, moving around people, seeking out the exit, she outshone everyone.

He'd created a trap for her which she'd had no choice but enter, circling into its center until he had her secure. Then why did he feel it was the other way around?

othing's changed.

Her words repeated in his mind as he stared at the papers which littered his desk—confidential bank statements, bills of lading, insurances—all designed to conceal the truth.

She was wrong. If what he suspected was true, then everything had changed. But there was only one way to know for sure because she'd tied up the truth behind a veil of paperwork and privacy screens which even he didn't have the power to uncover. His only hope of knowing the truth was for her to tell him.

The draft from the overhead fan lifted the pages through which Zavian sifted as if they were light things of no importance. But they were of the utmost importance, Zavian thought. They had the power to change his life. He placed a heavy glass paperweight on the pile with careful deliberation. If only he could contain his thoughts as easily. He sat back and let his head rest against the leather of the office chair.

The whirr of the fan and the splash of water from the fountain outside his office should have had a soothing effect.

But they did nothing to ease the tension which gnawed at his temples. Nothing to pacify the roaring sound in his brain that had sprung up at the sight of the signature on the museum's ownership records of the prize of its collection. It wasn't that it was her name, it was that everyone who'd been traced who bore that name had had nothing to do with the purchase and donation of the piece back to his country. Someone wanted to be anonymous. And who else but Gabrielle would have both the knowledge, the money, and a reason?

He took a deep breath, pushed the chair away from the table and walked over to the floor-to-ceiling windows which overlooked the city's old quarter. At that moment, the sun rose behind the soft-edged minarets and mosques of a city steeped in its medieval origins. His grandfather had preferred this office, and when Zavian succeeded his father to the throne, he'd immediately made it his.

And somehow, the setting was an appropriate one for what he believed he'd uncovered. The museum—whose outline he could see facing one side of the civic square, hidden by palm trees—had acquired the jewel in its crown of antiquities when the Khasham Qur'an had been anonymously donated.

He sighed and closed his eyes. *Gabrielle.* The name escaped his lips like a puff of warm desert wind, like a memory of a kiss. Only Gabrielle would believe that she could trick him. Nowhere else in this city would anyone have dared, or have imagined it were possible to—what was that quaint English expression?—pull the wool over the eyes of their sheikh and king. But Gabrielle had. He'd underestimated her. It seemed *that* was mutual.

There was a subdued knock at the door, followed by his vizier's entrance. Naseer was the only person allowed to enter his rooms without awaiting his response.

The elderly vizier gave a slight bow and approached him. "Your Majesty."

Zavian turned his back on the rising sun, which cast a long shadow across the room. "Naseer, did you check with the museum?"

"I did. Although the museum's director was confused as to why you'd want to know this before sunrise."

Zavian glared at Naseer. He could hardly tell him that his obsession with Gabrielle was only increasing over time. While he managed to push her to the shadowy recesses of his mind during the day, she always emerged fully formed in his imagination at night. "And what did he say?"

"The piece was purchased from the dealer for a rumored one million dollars, and has been donated to the museum. He wanted to assure you that it was all above board, that everything has been done legally."

Zavian looked out at the museum, its honey-colored stone warming now under the slowly moving finger of sunlight. "And the paper trail your source provided"—he nodded to the pile of papers on his desk—"is genuine?"

Naseer gave a slight bow, which was for form only. "I am assured it is."

Zavian let the remaining doubt burn away just as the sun burned away the shreds of mist that lingered along the coast, leaving the full form of his golden city revealed. Its domed minarets thrust up into the pale gold-gray sky, the warmth of its umber tones deepening, minute by minute, in the early morning light.

Naseer sniffed with disapproval. "Although I haven't seen the papers myself, as you instructed."

"Indeed."

"Do you care to tell me what this is about?" his vizier asked. "The museum director isn't the only one who's curious."

Zavian shook his head. "It's of no consequence." Not to his vizier, anyway. But to Zavian? It had the power to change his world.

"I hadn't realized you were so interested in the museum's acquisition process."

Why did Zavian keep the old man around? He was a thorn in his side. But as he'd practically raised him, he couldn't imagine living without him, no matter how irritating, or dismissive he was of Zavian's word. Where others would quake at Zavian's merest glance, Naseer would answer him back. Trouble was, it was usually a pertinent answer—an answer, or a question, that no one else dared give and that Zavian knew, deep down, he needed to hear.

"You're surprised I like culture, Naseer?"

The old man raised his eyebrow. "The nearest you've ever come to culture was hunting in the desert with your grandfather's spears, or the harness on your Arab stallions when you raced."

"Ah, a blend of tradition and sport. Yes, you're probably right. But it's never too late to start, is it? Never too late to show the world that my country is more than simply a producer of oil and a strategically placed ancient port. Maybe it is time to attract more tourists here. Tourists who, in turn, will bring investment from foreign companies. Under our control, of course."

"Of course." There was a moment of silence while they both remembered when that *hadn't* been the case. It had taken a great deal of work to redress the wrongs his great-grandfather had innocently created.

"Besides, it's the PR and marketing that you've always told me I should be more interested in, right?"

Naseer nodded thoughtfully. "It's certainly timely. With the bi-millennial celebration coming up as well as your, er, personal plans, a renewed focus on public relations can do nothing but good for you and Gharb Havilah." He said the name of his country softly, with a reverence that betrayed his love for it. However he treated his king and subjects, Zavian knew his vizier would do whatever he had to do for his country. Naseer nodded to the city. "Two thousand years, Zavian. Two *thousand* years."

Zavian looked at the old man, whose expression revealed the emotion that had made him call Zavian by his first name, something he rarely did. "A milestone worth celebrating indeed."

"A personal one, as well as state one. Marriage negotiations are about to commence with the King of Tawazun between you and the eldest daughter."

Zavian grunted, and Naseer frowned.

"You agreed."

"I did. Now that King Amir has married, the task has fallen to me."

"I'm sure it won't be an unpleasant one. The princess is reputed to be very beautiful."

Gabrielle's image refused to be replaced by that of the Tawazun princess. He had reasons to delay his decision, but he had only one which prevented him—Gabrielle.

He was waiting for the day when his heart wouldn't ache for her, when he wouldn't feel her betrayal as sharply as a stab in the back. And that day was drawing closer. When he'd discovered the mystery behind the identity of the donor of the fabulous centerpiece to the collection, and how much the donor had paid for it, he knew Gabrielle was behind it. Not only because she was one of the few who'd have been able to confirm its provenance, but also because of the price.

A million dollars had been given to Gabrielle to stay away from him and his country by his father. She'd taken it and left Gharb Havilah. And someone had paid the exact same sum for a piece of Gharb Havilah's culture. If it *was* her, it proved she didn't want the money in the first place. Then why did she take it? He had his suspicions but was looking forward to finding out the answer from her.

"I've arranged a meeting with the King of Tawazun."

Zavian nodded. "When?"

"Two weeks."

"Good. That will give me time."

"Time?" His vizier narrowed his gaze. Zavian knew that look of old. Sometimes he thought Naseer knew him better than he knew himself. "Time for what? That girl?"

Zavian ground his teeth. He'd always hated his vizier's antipathy to Gabrielle. "You mean Dr. Taylor?"

"Of course I mean her. I was against you bringing her here, and I was right. She's unsettling you. I can't believe you want her here after what she did."

"It was just money."

"Just a million dollars, which was paid to her to leave you. She needed no persuading."

Zavian looked at his vizier suddenly. "And how would you know that?"

The vizier's glance slid away. "I heard."

Not for the first time Zavian wondered what part his vizier had played in Gabrielle's disappearance.

"Anyway, it's irrelevant. You know now that she's the sort of woman who can be bribed, she's not loyal, she's not for you, and she's not for our country."

Zavian no longer believed anything of the sort, but decided to play things close to his chest. The three countries which comprised the ancient land of Havilah needed to unite with Tawazun through blood ties, and his own country needed a queen in whom his people could believe. With a history of bitter battles over the centuries for control of the strategic port, his country had now entered a period of peace, and he would do all he could to ensure that continued.

And that meant building up a common identity, and a people loyal to the Crown.

"I know what kind of queen my country needs. It needs someone who believes in it utterly, and who will be loyal to it, absolutely."

The vizier nodded, not noticing any shortcomings in Zavian's statement. "Exactly. It needs a Tawazun princess."

Zavian didn't reply.

GABRIELLE RAN her fingers lightly over the objects of her passion, which, growing up, had been more familiar to her than dolls, before pushing the tray back into the cabinet. After spending a morning in meetings with the museum director and his team, she'd managed to secure a whole afternoon alone with some of the country's most precious artifacts. She'd told him she needed time to inspect each piece personally and its data. It wasn't exactly true, and she suspected the director knew it. But it seemed either he didn't mind or had been told to give her free rein. She suspected the latter.

She glanced around the room at the ancient pottery shards, at the fragments of ornate tiles and rare, intact pieces in their display cases. The pieces, which illuminated the everyday life of the Bedouin a thousand years earlier, were her whole life. At the age of three, her grandfather had pushed a soft brush into her hands to sweep away the sand from buried objects. As an impressionable girl, she'd lain in her tent at night, moved by the songs, poetry, and music of the Bedouin who continued to live their tribal lives as they had done for centuries in the desert. And then later she'd developed a career which had extended beyond the desert, all the way through to the hallowed halls of Oxford. She might have left it a year ago, but there was no denying that Gharb Havilah and its people and culture were her life.

And, while she worked tirelessly towards these artifacts receiving international recognition for their cultural significance and artistry, her life in the desert had taught her one other thing. It had ingrained in every pore of her skin, in every pulse of her blood through her body—her need for freedom. Being confined to the palace was killing her.

Reluctantly, she locked away the last piece and gave the windowless room one last sweeping glance. She'd be staying there, working through the evening surrounded by her favorite objects if she could have her way. But there was only one person who could do as they wished in Gharb Havilah, and that was the king. And he'd again summoned her to meet him. But it wasn't a public reception this time. It was dinner. She just hoped there would be plenty of other people seated between her and Zavian.

ZAVIAN SAT ALONE in the grand dining room, its mahogany table polished, reflecting the wrought gold lamps overhead. The darting flames of candles—caught by the breeze flowing in through the open doors—cast moving shadows over the ceiling. The door opened, and he rose instinctively to meet her. He'd arranged this meeting, but nothing could have prepared him for seeing her again. He devoured every detail of her hungrily with his eyes, needing to know her again.

She hesitated at the entrance and looked around as the door was closed behind her. She glanced around the room at his servants, who stood at each of the four corners of the room, ready to jump to his command and provide for his every need. He was accustomed to it, but he noted the wariness in her blue eyes, which were colorless in the candlelight.

He flexed his hands, forcing himself not to go to her, not

to take her in his arms, because in that one moment before speech, before anything else, there was only them. And he wanted her, just as he always had.

Then she looked away, and he remembered everything that had happened. Their passion, her rejection. Simple, final. Or so she'd thought. But she was unfinished business for him, business he *had* to finish before he could move on with the last piece of the jigsaw that was his life. Before he married and had a family. He wanted her, he would have her, and only then could he continue with his life.

He rubbed his fingers together before extending his hand to her, his body and head remaining rigid and composed. "Gabrielle."

She walked the length of the table, her large eyes never leaving his. She looked at his hand and then held his gaze once more. She didn't take his hand. An insult he was not accustomed to, an insult he would not forgive lightly.

"Why have you brought me here?" she asked. Her voice trembled, but the jut of her chin and fierce eyes revealed it shook through anger, not nerves. She'd never been able to hide her feelings. They flitted across her face as openly as the shadows and wind upon the desert sands.

He indicated the food before them, deliberately misunderstanding her question. "To dine with your new employer, of course. Please, take a seat."

She hesitated only briefly before taking her seat, sensibly realizing she had no choice. She looked smaller than he remembered, fragile against the large-framed mahogany chairs he'd inherited from his great-grandfather's extravagant reign. She'd lost weight. He hadn't expected that. He'd held the image of her twelve months ago in his head ever since she'd left. But time hadn't stood still.

He nodded to his butler who stood at the door, and suddenly the doors were opened, and trays of steaming food were brought in and served, and their wine glasses were filled with the best French white wine, which he knew was her favorite.

"Just like old times, Gabrielle," he couldn't help teasing. He had her where he wanted her now, and he could afford to relax a little.

She looked around at his staff, whose presence he scarcely registered anymore. "Hardly," she muttered.

He frowned and followed her gaze. He signaled to his servants to leave the room. After the door closed with a subtle click, leaving them entirely alone, he turned to her.

"Is that better?"

He could see the struggle in her gaze. "I didn't mean for you to dismiss them."

"Then what did you mean?"

"I was merely pointing out how you've changed."

He sat back in his chair and carefully placed his wine glass onto the table, giving himself time for his irritation to fade. It didn't. "I am now King of Gharb Havilah, *not* second in line to the throne. My father is dead, as is my elder brother. Of course I have changed. As have you. But not enough. I'd have preferred it if you'd changed more." And he meant it. If she'd changed beyond recognition, grown stouter, dyed her hair, assumed the latest fashions, he might not have felt that same slam of lust in his gut. But even as the thought entered his mind, he dismissed it. Deep down, he knew that no amount of change would affect how much he needed her. And it was this he had to remedy. Twelve months of separation had made no difference. He hoped one month's togetherness would exorcise her hold over him.

"I assumed you didn't invite me to dine purely to insult me."

"You assume correctly."

"Then why?"

"Why are you here?" He needed to stall her. "I wish to dine with my new employee." He opened his arms in a gesture of innocence. "Is that so surprising?"

Her eyes darkened with annoyance. "Yes, it is. I was under the impression my contract had been organized by the museum director, that I was *his* employee. I hardly expected to dine with the king."

"The museum director," he repeated. "Really?" He shook his head. "No, Gabrielle, it was I. But you deviated from my plans. Instead of coming direct, you took the plane to Dubai, and then came overland through the hinterland and Tawazun. Your old haunts."

"You know which route I took," she replied slowly, shaking her head.

"Of course. How could you think I wouldn't?"

He speared a forkful of the spiced lamb and forced himself to eat, indicating that she should do the same. She sat forward, and he noticed her nostrils flare with appreciation at the aroma from the pungent spices. Despite her unwillingness to dine with him, she was being seduced by the traditional feast of Bedouin delicacies he'd ordered.

"Please," he said. "Begin." His heart softened at her hesitation and the uncertainty in her eyes. "It is tradition, Gabrielle, when we welcome old friends into our country, to share our food. I apologize if my welcome lacks polish, but, as you will undoubtedly remember, I am more a man of action than words."

She bit her lip, nodded once, and broke off a piece of the traditionally baked *regag* bread. He sat back with a sigh. Her defenses had slipped a notch, and he felt a hurdle had been overcome. She took a sip of water and he watched as her lips, not painted, but softly wet from the water, enveloped the fork upon which she'd speared a piece of lamb and aubergine. Her eyes closed momentarily as the tastes and spices of the dish bloomed on her tongue. He sipped his wine to hide the effect her eating was having on him.

"You like the food?" he asked, after he'd had a chance to recover.

She swallowed and nodded with a smile. "Yes, indeed. Thank you for the welcome and the dinner. It's appreciated."

One question hovered on his lips. He ignored it. It was too soon.

"It's always a pleasure to provide things for people who truly appreciate them." He shifted in his seat. He'd imagined that by placing Gabrielle at the end of the table, he'd be safe from her allure. He'd been wrong.

Her smile widened, and she raised her eyebrows in mild surprise. "I do. I'd almost..." She trailed off.

"Forgotten?" he prompted. "I can't believe that."

Her smile quirked briefly. "No. I don't think I'll ever forget this place." She looked around. "It's in my blood."

He sucked in a satisfied breath. She'd given him what he wanted. It was what he hoped she'd say, it was what he'd believed she'd say, but what he hadn't known was whether she understood it herself. He could proceed with confidence.

And he did. He made sure she relaxed and enjoyed the food and kept the conversation on the impersonal—about the country, archaeology, and mutual friends. Until finally, only the remnants of the meal lay between them, and the candles had burned low, one of them sending sputtering shadows across her face.

"Zavian." She sat back in her chair, cradling a glass of wine in her hands. "I asked you a question at the beginning of dinner which you refused to answer directly. I'll ask it again." She cocked her head to one side, in an attitude he found impossibly appealing. "Why have you brought me here?"

"I thought we should meet as soon as possible to overcome any slight"—he hesitated as he contemplated which word to choose—"awkwardness. After all, you will be working, and living, close to me."

He didn't think she could have paled any more under the warm lights.

"Close to you…" she said faintly.

"Indeed. Your work will be the jewel in the crown of our forthcoming celebrations. I wish to oversee it, to make sure everything is as it should be."

"You have people who do that. This *is* business, isn't it?" Her eyes glittered, and he suddenly felt unsure. Her eyes were shadowed as if she were hiding from him. "What else do you expect from me?"

He tilted his head back. "You think I've brought you here to renew our relationship?"

"I have no idea. You've orchestrated this whole thing, that much is clear. You don't need me to work for the bi-millennial celebrations. They've been planned for months, years probably. They're happening in one month. It's a deadline. But for what?"

He licked his lips, as much at the sight of her flushed cheeks as at the unexpected clear summary of the situation. He liked the way she challenged him. It had always been that way. He'd set something in motion, like a chess game, expecting a particular result. Still, he could never predict the unique combination of her intelligent and emotional response, so different to his own. It had kept him on his toes then, and it looked as if it would do the same now. He smiled.

"A deadline signifying a new Gharb Havilah, new beginnings, the end of the old."

"You're getting married, aren't you? You've brought me here to rekindle something before you marry?"

He grunted an unamused laugh. Sometimes her perspicacity could be downright annoying. But he knew how to

33

silence that sharp intellect, he knew how to subdue her. He rose from his chair, the legs grating against the stone-flagged floor, and stepped towards her. She looked up at him with startled eyes. He didn't even need to touch her. She leaned back, gripping the table, and he watched that long neck swallow convulsively. He longed to kiss it. But he refused to indulge the impulse. No matter what she might think, he wasn't going to take anything that wasn't willingly given. But a small reminder of their chemistry was no bad thing.

His eyes roamed her face, re-acquainting his mind, his senses with her. "Maybe that's wishful thinking?"

She couldn't speak; she looked stunned. She shook her head in denial.

He raised a disbelieving eyebrow. "No? Are you sure about that?"

She shook her head again, repeating the movement, unaware that she was answering the opposite of her intention.

He grunted softly and stepped away. "Go now. Sleep well."

He didn't wait for her response. Instead, he opened the door for her where an assistant was waiting, and watched as she took a deep breath, rose, and walked to the door. She stopped beside him. "Nothing's changed, Zavian. Nothing." She continued through the door, and he closed it behind her with more force than he'd intended.

It wouldn't take long to seduce her, because she was indeed mistaken. Everything had changed, and she wanted him as much as he wanted her.

AS IF IN A DAZE, Gabrielle followed the assistant back to her suite of rooms. From the moment Zavian had stepped close to her, her body had betrayed her. It had dulled her mind until all she was aware of was him—his physicality, and desire for her. She couldn't even remember what he'd asked her, all she'd been aware of were those narrow lips of his which others had always pronounced stern, but which she knew could create magic. His voice had played her senses, just as it ever had, his velvety rich tones vibrating to her core. His eyes had looked inside her and found her. She breathed deeply, trying to quiet her quickened heartbeat, seeking to extinguish the arousal that simply being with him had sparked back into life. Dammit, *she'd* sparked back into life.

She kept on walking, one foot in front of the other, her footsteps ringing out on the marble floor. She had only one month to endure, one month to keep herself safe from this man who'd trapped her simply to amuse himself, to retaliate for the fact that she'd left him. One month before she could free herself from this man whose future she could be no part of.

CHAPTER 3

*G*abrielle scrolled through the list of bullet points in the email she'd received from the king's office. Her work had been reduced to distinct black marks—like dark circles caused by gunshots—one after another, after another. It fitted somehow. Zavian was determined to show that no one took control of him, not his family, not his subjects, and not, apparently, his ex-lovers. Control by bullet point.

She scrolled back to the top of the list. Number one had been ticked off already. Planning meetings with the museum staff around the arrangements for the bi-millennial celebrations. It seemed she was hardly required for that. Everything was in hand, which brought her to number two. Now, this was a bit trickier. It had been decided—by whom, she didn't know—that the exhibits needed more than simple dry descriptions. They needed stories giving their background and cultural significance, stories that would appeal internationally to the general public and which would make the pieces come alive.

Again, this was mostly in hand. Except for three pieces

which had been earmarked for her. The Khasham Qur'an, pottery from an area in the desert which she and her grand-father had excavated, and a collection of poetry.

She sat back with a sigh, nibbling her fingertips as she contemplated why Zavian had selected these items for her alone. Because she did not doubt that he was behind this. Poetry, she could handle. She'd been raised by her poetry-loving grandfather and had helped him with his research. Pottery? Again, it wouldn't be a stretch. She was more familiar with ancient Havilah pottery than the pots and pans in her small Oxford apartment. But what would be a stretch —a *total* stretch—was the Khasham Qur'an. There was nothing she didn't know about it. And there was no way she could share all she knew with anyone, least of all, Zavian.

She sighed and tossed a pen onto the table. She closed her eyes and groaned. She couldn't do it. It had been a spur of the moment decision to buy the Qur'an when it had come up for sale at auction in London. She'd pre-empted the auction with an offer which the owner—a dealer who'd preferred to take the offer than risk scrutiny for a higher price—had accepted with alacrity. As far as she was concerned, there was only one place the Khasham Qur'an should be, and that was in Gharb Havilah. She knew she could have purchased it for less, given the shady dealings of the seller. Still, she wanted the money she'd accepted from Zavian's father to be gone from her account. She'd taken it for one purpose only— to convince Zavian that he should leave her alone. His country needed him, it didn't need her. If she'd done as he'd wanted and stayed with him, it could have destroyed his country.

But it was her weakness in buying the Qur'an and returning it to its place of birth, which had found her out.

She jumped as the shrill ring of her phone broke her concentration. She peered at the screen. Few people knew she was here, but the screen revealed the caller was unlisted. She tapped the screen reluctantly.

"Hello?"

"Gabrielle." Zavian's easily recognizable voice spoke her name as if identifying her for the first time.

"Zavian," she replied, with equal force. He hesitated a moment, and she suddenly realized that few people would call him by his given name, now that his close family had died. Her heart softened despite her intentions. "Was there something you wanted?" she added, in a more conciliatory tone.

"A meeting. With you. Now."

"Hm," she grunted, pulling the phone from her ear and looking at it briefly in surprise. She tapped the screen so she could hear him more clearly, wondering if she'd imagined the peremptory tone. "I'm sorry, I didn't quite get that."

She distinctly heard the sharp intake of breath. "Gabrielle." Her name rushed out on his breath, and she could have sworn she felt it tickle her skin. "A meeting in my office to discuss your work... if you'd be so kind," he said, in a threatening undertone, which completely negated his words.

She folded an arm over her chest. "Of course, Your Majesty. I am yours to command," she said, realizing her ironic tone was completely disregarded as she heard only the empty silence of the discontinued call.

He'd ordered her to him and had immediately hung up. What kind of man did that? She jumped up and glanced out the window in the direction of his office. But she knew the answer. A king, an autocrat, someone accustomed to being obeyed absolutely—this wasn't the man she knew.

For a split second, she contemplated remaining in her office, considered *not* obeying the summons. But only for a second, because she soon foresaw what would happen.

Humiliation as he—or his staff—came for her. She rose and shook her head. She couldn't stand much more of this.

She'd arrived in Gharb Havilah, intending to hide what she'd done for as long as possible. But, she now realized, that would only protract things. She checked her reflection in the mirror. No, she just might do the opposite of what he expected, to put him off his guard and to get herself out of here.

Gabrielle unhooked her abaya and scarf, which she always had ready on the back of her door. While women could wear what they liked inside the palace, the majority tended to wear variations of the abaya and scarf to meetings and outside in the city. Besides, she felt at her most comfortable in them.

When she opened her door, she found a security guard was waiting to take her to Zavian. They walked along a path beneath a colonnade providing shelter from the mid-day sun. The days were sweltering under the mid-summer sun. But the trickle of water never ceased, and the plants appeared immaculate, lush, and restful to the eye. Small birds flittered among the large vase-shaped flowers sucking the nectar before flying away, scarcely larger than an insect. Gabrielle had missed the beauty of this world. Its over-abundance, exuberance, and shimmering mystery and exoticism. For all of Oxford's beauty, it seemed gray and lifeless after such a place as this, more ancient even than medieval Oxford.

As they moved through the palace corridors, the guard refused to converse with her, despite her many attempts. Instead, she found herself following his quick steps to a part of the palace she'd only ever been once before. The security guard stopped at a door.

She shook her head. "But this is the way to the—" Before

she could finish her sentence, the guard opened the door to reveal a private study which was empty.

He smiled politely and left the room. She looked around, suddenly nervous. A large desk stood before the window, designed, no doubt, to awe the person entering the room. Apart from the walls of books, an informal space of two sofas and a couple of chairs surrounding a table completed the furniture. The last and only time she'd been here was when Zavian's father had summoned her. It had been his private study, and was, no doubt, now his son's.

She stood still, looking around, waiting for pieces of the puzzle to fall into place. Why had Zavian called her to this room to discuss work? Or was it a ruse simply to get her here? She drew in a calming breath, and then her eyes settled on a cabinet to one side. It was small and, from a glance, appeared to hold only a few select pieces.

But she knew their shape.

She'd been with Zavian when they'd found them. The memories shot at her like arrows piercing her veneer of protection. Without that defense, she felt the full force of that moment eighteen months ago, when she'd been alone with Zavian in the desert. The excitement of the find was eclipsed only by the lovemaking afterward. She closed her eyes against the full force of emotions, which rose like a tidal wave from deep inside her.

Suddenly she felt a prickle down her neck and back, which settled low inside. The silk of her abaya shimmered slightly as the air shifted. A door clicked closed, and she swung around. Zavian was formally dressed in a white robe, which made him appear even taller than he was. She'd always loved the traditional robes. They had a simplicity and a beauty which was timeless. Every eye in the room moved to Zavian when he wore European clothes, but the clothes of a king? He was not only magnetic, but awesome. This wasn't a man to cross. This wasn't *her* man any longer, not the man with whom she'd discovered the objects.

The prickle that had begun in her neck sunk lower into her gut as Zavian walked towards her.

"Zavian!" His name slipped from her lips before she could check it. She could feel the color rushing to her cheeks as he gazed at her with a hunger which made her feel weak. She couldn't be sucked in by it, to forget why they could never be together. Somehow she found the control and stepped away, needing space between them. "Your Majesty."

As she uttered the honorific, the look in his eyes changed, and the arrogant control that she'd witnessed on the first night returned.

"Dr. Taylor."

His formality cut to the heart of her, but she refused to allow him to see it. As far as he was concerned she'd been bribed to leave him and his country, and she'd disappeared from his life without a farewell.

"I see you've been admiring some pieces from my private collection."

She gasped as he lifted his hand and reached past her. She froze, all her senses acutely attuned to him, wondering what he was going to do. But he simply retrieved one of the objects she'd been looking at and held it up to the light, twisting it in his strong hands, hands whose sensitivity she remembered well.

"I admire this piece for its simplicity."

Taking advantage of his switch in focus, she exhaled lightly and composed herself. "I... I've never considered it to be simple."

The corners of his lips tweaked slightly, but he didn't shift his gaze from the piece. "Its contours are regular, its shape standard for its type. How could it *not* be considered simple?" he asked, passing it to her, their fingers touching.

"Because…" She paused, willing herself to focus on the piece, not him. "Because every time I look at it, I see something different." She twisted the piece in the light. "A shade, a line, a ridge, a measurement of time etched into its fabric. Something beautiful, and yet flawed, all together in one piece."

She looked from the piece to him. He'd lowered his eyes, which were now focused on her lips. When he raised them again, their chestnut hue was darker than before. "You always did make something simple, complex."

"Perhaps because it was never simple."

A muscle flickered in his jaw, but he said nothing. "You're wrong. Everything is simple. Everything can be reduced to essentials."

"Why is that so important to you?"

"Because only then can you judge it, only then can you assess it for what it is."

He was too near for her to think clearly. His eyes roamed her face as the silence lengthened, deepened, and became unbearable. She swallowed and stood a little straighter.

"Well, I wish you luck with that. What is it you wanted to see me about, Your Majesty?" She hoped by using his title she'd remind them both that the intimacy of their conversation needed to stop.

"I paid a lot of money to bring you here, and yet you demand to know why I wish to meet you?" His eyes hooded, and he cocked his head a little to one side. "I thought you knew all about the power of money."

She wished she didn't blush so easily, but his comment sent the blood pulsing through her, branding her with guilt. But there was nothing she could do to defend herself. She needed to be guilty in his eyes. "Indeed."

"And the person with the money has the control, isn't that so?"

She nodded. His proximity was making it hard for her to think straight. "Sometimes," she muttered.

"I think you'll find it's true all the time. Otherwise, why would you be here?"

"But why me? Others could have done this job. Others without the complications I bring."

"Sometimes, unfortunately, complications cannot be avoided. They have to be faced to make things simple once more. There are things, Gabrielle, I need to know. Beginning with this." He picked up a remote control and pressed a button. A part of the wall slid away, revealing the Khasham Qur'an.

Stunned, she stepped back as if pushed by a force field. She'd assumed it had been locked away somewhere in the most secure part of the museum. She'd assumed wrong. She was faced with her weakness—a way to absolve herself from accepting the bribe, a way to return a treasure to its rightful place, a way she'd thought had been anonymous.

Maybe it was fake? She walked up to it, heartbeat quickening, but could see at a glance it was genuine. While the binding was more recent—echoing the ochre and brilliant indigo of the pages within the book itself—there was no doubting the gilded angular Kufic script, laid down using a solution in which gold was suspended. And, as she cocked her head to one side, the uneven pages which carried the discoloration of centuries confirmed it. She closed her eyes and drew in a breath—despite the glass case in which it lay, she knew its smell. She'd held it and knew the musty aroma of antiquity and desert.

It all proved it was the original, which meant someone had linked her to it. She swallowed down the lump which had appeared from nowhere and blinked back the tears. The Qur'an was set well. The background was the bleached stone color of the hammada plains, and the light above it was clear, revealing everything there was to be seen in the illuminated decorations of the most valuable Qur'an to come out of Gharb Havilah. But not so bright as to damage the piece, which she knew had lain hidden near a cave for a thousand years, buried alongside the king who'd ordered its creation. She knew this because her grandfather had told her often enough about how he'd discovered it and how subsequently it had gone missing. Missing until six months ago when it had reappeared and she'd bought it. The note on the piece identified the donor as anonymous.

When she looked back at Zavian, his eyes had changed. He knew. He absolutely knew. *He* might be inscrutable, but *she* was an open book to him. He motioned her to sit at the table, in front of the Khasham Qur'an. She had no option but to do so, to sit and look at the object which had betrayed her.

He stood beside her. "It's beautiful, isn't it?"

"Yes," she said, from between tight lips.

"And mysterious."

She twisted her lips closed as if scared the truth would come tumbling out.

"Don't you agree?"

"Not really. We know where it came from."

"Yes, but we don't know how it came here, do we?"

She shrugged. "I don't see how I can help you." She kept her eyes firmly on him, refusing to give him the satisfaction of looking away. Still, all the while knowing that her bright red cheeks betrayed her.

"Do you not?"

She shrugged. "The provenance is well known."

"Not to me."

"It was found not far from here, I believe."

"Among the ruins of Khasham. Yes, thank you. *That* much, I do know."

"And then it went missing."

"I'm so pleased that I spent so much money to bring you here, to receive such an incisive background to the piece. Although I'm not sure your Oxford college will be as pleased."

The reminder that the future of her Oxford college, together with its staff, depended on her work, was timely. She swallowed. "What else do you want to know?"

He casually indicated the Qur'an. "I've told you. About the Qur'an. I want you to tell me what happened to it. I wish to know how it came to be part of my collection." He sat down, frowning, his hands steepled before him.

She opened her mouth to speak, but the words eluded her.

"Tell me," he repeated.

"I can't."

"I thought you might say that. But I've thought of a way to be helpful to you."

"Helpful?" she repeated weakly, hardly able to think straight.

"Indeed. I've cleared my schedule for the next twenty-four hours to assist you in this regard."

"You... what?"

"I thought you might find your memory faulty, and I've decided to help you out."

"So thoughtful," she murmured.

"I simply want the truth."

"And if I can't discover the truth?"

"Then, your Oxford college will not receive payment for your services and will cease to exist."

"How do you know—"

"That your college is desperately short of funds? It came to my attention that one of its major sources of funds had dried up."

She closed her eyes briefly. "It was you."

He shrugged. "I do what I have to do." He stepped away. "Be ready in an hour."

"Where are we going?"

"I anticipated you might be reluctant to tell me." He took another step away. "We're going to the desert castle of Khasham."

"The desert castle," she repeated. She shook her head. "But—"

He turned to her, his face hard. "No buts. We're going to Khasham. Once back in the surroundings where it all began, perhaps then you'll find it easier to tell me everything I wish to know. And if you don't? Then I shall remain by your side for the duration of your contract." He paused, but she didn't answer. "You have a month, Gabrielle. One month until the bi-millennial celebrations, when your paid services will no longer be required."

"Why then?"

"Because I will then know exactly what I need to know."

As he swept out the room, she knew with absolute certainty that he wouldn't allow her to leave Gharb Havilah without giving him what he wanted. But, if she did that, she risked damaging the very country she loved.

As ZAVIAN WALKED along the palace corridors to his suite of offices, he had only one image held in his mind, triggered by the way the rose-colored light had touched her face. It had been soon after her grandfather had died. The same light had fallen on her face as she'd awoken in a traditional Bedouin tent in the desert, far from civilization. He'd opened a flap of the tent so he could watch the sun slowly rise through the trunks of the palms, shimmering its delicate peachy rays across the water onto the oasis where birds had come to drink before the heat soared. But he'd had no interest in the wildlife that day. Only the way the shadows of the palm leaves had flickered light across her face, relaxed by sex and sleep. He'd known at that moment that she would always be his, no matter what.

Growing up, he'd got to know Gabrielle's grandfather on his frequent visits to the palace to visit his own grandfather. He'd always sought the older man out to listen to tales of the desert and the history of his country, about which none of his own family appeared particularly concerned. And he'd heard all about Gabrielle long before he'd ever met her. That meeting hadn't happened until they were both teenagers. But they hadn't come close until an accidental meeting in the desert when she'd returned from her studies at Oxford University.

Her grandfather had died shortly after their relationship had begun. Zavian had taken it slowly at first, knowing her grief over losing her only relative. But, if he was correct about her role in the repatriation of the Khasham Qur'an, then her reason for accepting the bribe from his father was called into question. Why had she taken it?

He thought he knew why, but he needed to hear it from her. And when he did, he'd resume his relationship with her, simply to rid himself of his obsession. That was all.

CHAPTER 4

*S*he'd never been good at being controlled. Not by a person or by a thing—a wall, a lock, an instruction. Her grandfather had known that, her head of department had come to realize that, but it seemed the King of Gharb Havilah had yet to learn it.

Yes, she wanted, no *needed* to go into the desert, but not with him. She wanted to be alone, now, more than ever before, free of the shackles of ownership, of locked doors, and deadlines. And, not least, free from Zavian's spell. Whenever she was near him, she wanted him, physically and emotionally, like a person emerging from the desert who'd survived only on meager rations. She was hungry and thirsty for him as if her life depended on it.

But it was no good. Despite all the lingering looks, theirs was a relationship with no future. Neither of them could deny their intense physical attraction to each other, nor their enjoyment in each other's company. She loved to watch Zavian's impassive face, noting the slight changes to indicate his humor, the slight contraction at the corner of his mouth when something amused him, and not least the heat in his eyes when he looked at her. But she had no choice but to resist the magnetic pull toward him. It could go nowhere because they were poles apart. And the thought of spending the next twenty-four hours—or longer—with him was enough to drive her crazy.

And she didn't intend to be driven crazy. That was why she'd arranged for a taxi to collect her a good two hours before the appointed time and to take her into the desert— not to the desert castle—but to the place she'd grown up with her grandfather. It would be deserted, she knew, but she needed to see it again, needed the solace just being in her old home would bring. She'd do what was required of her, she reasoned. She didn't need physical resources to put together the PR stories; it was all in her head and her laptop. She'd be working, keeping to the letter of her contract, just not quite in the way Zavian imagined. He might be king, but he wasn't her king.

She packed her bag and arrived at the car early, handing her bag to the chauffeur, who stowed it away. She was about to get into it when a group of men burst out from the castle. She knew it was him before she saw him. Athletic, white-robed men talked into microphones and swept the empty courtyard with their gaze. Only one gaze was directed at her —the man at their center.

She jumped in the car. "Let's go! Now!" she called to the driver. But the driver pretended not to hear and stepped to one side, allowing a clear view of Zavian striding out of the white marble foyer of the palace, flanked either side by security, his eyes focused on her beneath a frown.

She looked away, steeling herself for his response.

"Good morning, Dr. Taylor," Zavian said, briefly gripping the top of the car and peering inside, looking over his dark glasses at her with eyes of obsidian. "It seems you anticipated we'd be making an early start."

She swallowed hard, then turned to him. "We? No. I was leaving on my own."

"And you were going to the desert castle?"

She shook her head and looked straight ahead. "I was going to my family home—my grandfather's house."

"To do what, exactly?"

"To work. As you wished me to do."

"What I wish is for us to proceed to the desert castle. Now is not the time for a sentimental return to your childhood home." He turned and issued a few short, sharp commands to his attendants, some of whom returned to the palace, while others jumped into cars which emerged at the wave of a hand. The sound of car doors slamming filled the courtyard. Zavian slid into the driver's seat and grunted with satisfaction as he handled the steering wheel and gear stick. He was in control, just as he liked it.

"Gabrielle," he said, not turning to look at her. "You should know I'm a man of my word. I said we'd go together, and that is what we'll do."

"And you have to drive, of course," she said, as his men stepped away from the car, leaving only the two of them inside. The gates rolled open, and Zavian drove through them, closely followed by two other vehicles.

He glanced at her. "Of course."

As they drove slowly through the old quarter and out toward the city boundary, she couldn't help remembering.

He glanced at her. "Although I seem to remember a time when you insisted on driving us around the desert in your grandfather's Jeep."

She looked at him, startled. It was as if he'd been reading her mind. "It was ancient and required gentle handling."

His glance set her pulse racing. Again, their minds were in sync. "And do you still think I don't know how to handle things gently when required?"

She swallowed but refused to answer. She risked a glance at his profile. Dark glasses screened his eyes from the sun as they burst out of the city and onto the short plain, which would take them to the mountain road and then to the desert interior.

"I grew up on horseback, remember," he continued. "To get the best out of an animal, one needs to know how to treat it—when to be gentle, when to be firm."

"But always to be in control," she murmured, as they passed lush farms, the result of heavy irrigation.

"Of course. One cannot change one's personality."

"More's the pity."

There was silence, and she glanced back at Zavian. He had one arm over the back of the seat, his hand nearly, but not quite touching her shoulder as he angled towards her. He looked less like a king now, and more like the man with whom she'd fallen in love. There was a sense of excitement in his eyes and something more.

He didn't need to stretch to extend his fingers to touch her shoulder if he desired. It seemed he didn't desire, not yet. "You would not like it if I changed my personality." A small smile played on his lips.

She shook her head and tried to suppress a smile. "You think you know me so well."

"I *do* know you." His finger now rested on her shoulder. "These past few days, I've watched you as you struggled to come to terms with the conditions at the palace, and yet you've enjoyed being back in Gharb Havilah."

There it was again—that contradiction. Her body buzzed at the thought that he'd watched, that he'd noticed her enjoyment and her discomfort at being trapped in the palace with him. But then, she felt like a rabbit caught in the glare of a headlight, unable to escape, stunned by the brightness of the light.

"Maybe." She focused studiously on the approaching line of mountains, which fringed the plain upon which the city sat.

His finger moved over her shoulder, and she closed her eyes against the sensation which was gentle, yet so powerful that it sent shivers snaking through her body to places where they really shouldn't snake.

"Gabrielle." His voice was hushed as if he, too, felt those same sensations. "You wanted to be free of the palace, and I am giving you this freedom."

She opened her mouth to speak, but the words wouldn't come. He truly believed he was giving her freedom. She could see it in his eyes. She shook her head, about to deny it, about to tell him that freedom couldn't be given. If it was, it was yet another form of control. But before she could speak, the hand on her shoulder caressed her again, and all thoughts fled.

"At dinner last night, you asked me a question, and I didn't answer."

She shrugged, not wanting an answer to that question right at that moment.

"You've forgotten? Then let me remind you. You asked me why I'd brought you here. You suggested I wished to rekindle something before I marry. And I didn't answer."

She smiled. "You seldom do, not if you don't want to."

"Ah, but it's not that I didn't want to, it's that I didn't know the answer. But now I do."

"What is it? What is the answer?"

"Later, I will show you later."

Show you, he said. Show, not tell. Her mind refused to shift from imagining *how* he would show her.

"Now," he continued, "tell me about the work you have been doing in Oxford."

She breathed a sigh of relief. She'd imagined he would

begin the inquisition over her involvement with the Qur'an immediately. Still, it seemed he was employing his self-described ability to tread gently to get results. Whatever, she was relieved.

The miles melted away as she talked about her work, on familiar ground once more. Her passion, her life's work. It wasn't until they were approaching the desert castle that he did more than merely prompt her with questions.

"You say this is your life's work." He gestured all around. "All of this. And yet you choose to live away from it."

The ease vanished instantly. She'd got carried away talking about her work and had fallen into his trap. "My work is academic, theoretical."

He glanced at her. "No, it's not. Otherwise, you wouldn't have done what you did."

"What do you mean?"

"You know perfectly well what I mean. You refuse to tell me the truth. But you will."

She bit her lip. "And how will you make me do that?"

She could feel his gaze rest on her briefly although she didn't meet it. She resolutely stared out the window at the castle, growing larger with each passing minute.

"I'll remind you of something."

"Remind?" she grunted. "That sounds very subtle."

"I can be. You, of all people, should know that." He paused. "Be quite sure, Gabrielle, you will tell me everything."

She swallowed. She did not doubt that he'd get his way in the end, but she was damned if she'd make it easy for him.

"Everything?" She drew in a deep, strengthening breath and turned in her seat to face him. She needed him to know that she wasn't afraid of him. "Everything could take us some time. Don't you have a country to run?"

"I do. And I will continue to run it from a distance while I find answers."

"Answers? To what questions."

Again a flick of those disdainful eyes. "You don't know?"

She shrugged. "Maybe one of the 'stories' you hired me to create?"

He didn't deign to respond to her suggestion, merely kept his eye on the road and, overtaking a car, sped off into the shimmering mirage of the desert road. He channeled all his frustration into the accelerator as they approached the castle gates, which opened to allow them to enter.

They drew up in a cloud of dust, far ahead of anyone else. The desert castle appeared deserted. Silence descended when he turned off the car's ignition.

"I want you to tell me why you took my father's money," Zavian said.

She hadn't expected him to be so direct. "I…"

"You *what?*" He sat forward. "Do you want to know why *I* think you took it?"

She shrugged stiffly. "I think that's obvious. Why do people usually take money?" She gritted her teeth together to stop herself trembling.

"There are many reasons." He jumped out of the car and walked around and opened the door for her. "The main reason is that they're greedy," he continued.

"Then that must be the reason here. Why wouldn't it be? I had little to my name. A million dollars can change a life."

He tilted his head to one side as if incredulous. "It can. But not yours." He looked at her with an expression that took her breath away. "I remember that abaya from a year ago when I bought it for you. You were always hopeless with clothes, unaware of them. It was one of the first things that struck me about you—your lack of interest in outward show. And I've seen the clothes you wear beneath it. British high street stores, if I am not mistaken."

She bridled with irritation. He'd always been such a snob.

"And how would you know that? Do you shop there often yourself?"

He didn't bother to respond. "So, I can only deduce that you didn't want the money for designer fashions."

The heat from the packed earth outside the umber colored stone of the desert palace rolled over her in waves. The smell of the desert scorched her lungs. She wanted to get out of the sun, into the shade and gardens that lay within. But she didn't dare back down.

"Of course not."

"Then what?"

"There are... there are plenty of other things in the world to buy besides clothes."

"Name them. Because I know for a fact, you've been living in one room at an Oxford University college since you left Gharb Havilah. And that came with the job. A bedsit, I believe?"

"It's convenient."

"Believe me. A luxury penthouse with maids is far more convenient."

"Maids," she scoffed. "What would I do with maids?"

"Indeed. You were always uncomfortable with them around." His face softened a little. "I recall you were always giving them days off."

She couldn't help but be seduced by the memory. "And I recall you were annoyed because they had work to do."

He paused. "Only for a while. You soon made me forget them."

The air thickened with memories, as the sunlight shimmered around them. Sweat beaded her forehead. He frowned.

Her chest tightened as her breathing came more rapidly. He seemed to be closer to her now. He cupped her cheek with the palm of his hand. It felt rough against her skin, prickling it and rousing it as he briefly caressed her cheek. She tried to shake her head, but he brought the other hand up to her other cheek, and she was trapped. And then she didn't want to escape anymore. The world was hushed as if waiting for his next move. Like the world, her senses were heightened and fixed only on him. He shook his head, and for a horrible moment, she thought he might step away. Instead, he moved closer to her. Her world darkened to the rich, inviting pools of his eyes as his lips touched hers. It was barely a kiss, a mere soft brush, and yet it had the most devastating effect. Her body reacted as if by an elastic memory, knowing at some deep level that this was her man. And then, as quickly as it had happened, he dropped his hands by his sides, as the cavalcade of security cars swept into the compound.

"Come, we can continue this inside the castle."

As his staff took themselves off to their quarters, she followed him inside the doors and into the cavernous main hall, which was the main reception room of the castle. She sat down on the nearest chair, and he closed the doors behind them. There were only the two of them in the ancient room—full of shadows and memories.

What had she just done? She'd shown him that she was his for the taking. She pushed her fingers through her hair, back from her face, focusing on taking calming breaths to quieten her raging body. Heat and moisture pulsed at the core of her, wanting him where he used to give her so much pleasure. She raised her palm to her cheek, where she could still feel that touch, not believing that her reactions could be so predictable.

He twisted around. "I apologize. I did not bring you here to kiss you."

She shook her head. "Then why did you bring me here?"

To her irritation, her voice was husky with desire, betraying her need.

He sucked in a long breath as if to counteract the effect her voice had on him. "Because I want to hear it from you."

"Hear what?" What was he talking about? Hear that she was still attracted to him? That her body still sung to the tune he played? That much must surely have been obvious.

He gripped the back of the chair. "I want to hear from you why you took my father's bribe. If it wasn't for what the money could do for your lifestyle, then why take it?"

She'd almost forgotten what they'd been talking about. All thoughts swept away by his devastating touch. "Because I... Because it's my business. Not yours."

Her response swept away the last remnants of their kiss, and he tilted his head back, his eyes narrowed as they shot a different kind of heat at her. "Really, Gabrielle? *Not* my business? Is that the best you can come up with? I suppose it is, because anything else and you'd have to reveal the truth."

"You seem to know so much. Perhaps *you* should tell *me* why I took the money."

He nodded, and she instantly regretted her words. "Because you wanted me to believe you could be bribed to leave me. That way you knew that I wouldn't come after you."

She closed her eyes briefly under the onslaught of bare truth. She shouldn't have done, because when she opened her eyes, she saw a light flash in his eyes as he realized his assertion was correct.

"Who's being too complex now?" she asked, trying to backtrack, trying to regain some element of control he was intent on robbing her of. "Money is money. Everyone needs it to survive."

"But not you, Gabrielle. You survive in that beautiful head of yours. Your material needs are minimal.

She bit her lip. "People change."

"Not you. I can see it in your eyes."

"I could have a manor house in the English countryside, for all you know."

"You could. But you haven't."

"Don't tell me, you've checked."

"Of course."

"Why would you bother investigating someone so disloyal, so easily bribed?"

"Because I didn't believe it when my father told me then, and I certainly don't believe it now. You wanted me to hate you, you wanted me not to follow you because you knew I would."

"You can think what you like."

"I do."

"Although I can't think why you imagine I would accept a bribe and then not spend the money."

"Oh, I don't think you haven't spent it." Electricity crackled in the air between them. "I *know* you have."

He couldn't. He might, for some reason, guess, but he couldn't know. She'd done everything to cover her traces. If there was one thing she knew about it was objects and ownership.

She shook her head. "Why would you think such a thing?"

"It's illegal for a foreign national to purchase an object of cultural interest in Gharb Havilah. But you know that, of course."

She refused to be drawn into the conversation. "What is that to do with me?"

"You bought the Qur'an in a private deal. A week later, the object was brought to Gharb Havilah and presented to the museum."

She shrugged. "Then I suggest you follow up with whoever brought it here."

"You know full well, that a courier company delivered it. A company that had no knowledge of who had sent it."

"Well, I fail to see why you believe I'm connected with this."

"*They* had no knowledge, but *I* made it my job to find out."

She'd had enough. She knew he'd never stop until he'd got what he wanted—her admission of guilt. He'd found out the truth somehow and was determined she should admit it. She swallowed. "How did you find out?"

The intensity had left his features as he sat back, now he'd got what he'd wanted. "I didn't, Gabrielle. It was merely a guess. True, it was an educated guess. That is why I wanted you here—to find out for myself the truth. I needed to know for certain."

"You tricked me."

"I did what I had to do to uncover the truth. And, I rather think it was you trying to trick me. You took the money from my father because you believed him when he told you that you would be no good for me and the future of my country. Isn't that so?"

She pursed her lips closed. He'd got what he wanted, and he wasn't going to get any more.

"And you only used it when you discovered the piece was for sale. You bought it and donated it anonymously to the country. Didn't you?"

His words filled the cavernous room, seeming to hang accusingly in the air. It seemed he wasn't going to relent until she'd given him an answer. "Yes."

He changed visibly before her eyes. It was as if a weight had been released from every muscle and sinew in his body. It was only then that she realized how much this meant to him. But it changed nothing. She'd simply have to find another way to show him that they had no future together.

He nodded and stopped pacing and sat on a chair opposite her. "So that leads us to another puzzle. Why would you spend a small fortune on a heritage collection which belongs to a foreign country?"

"Why, because it's important."

"For us, maybe. But for you? You're not one of us, are you?"

It was as if she'd been struck. He was right. She wasn't one of his people, she wasn't of this country, but she felt like one. He leaned forward, with passion. They were close to each other.

"I ask you again, Gabrielle, why did you take my father's money and spend it on this object if you are not one of us? If you'd simply wanted to rid yourself of the money you could have donated it to any number of charities, but you didn't. You spent it on an object of national significance to the country."

She opened her mouth to speak, but no words emerged. He was asking too much of her; he was asking her questions that she'd never dared ask herself.

"You're right. It was stupid of me."

He sat back, defeated. "You're not stupid."

"Then what am I?"

"Misguided. Ignorant of the fact that you belong to this country as much as anyone. You are one of us, whether you like it, or believe it, or not." He sighed and looked at the floor for a few moments, and when he looked back up at her, his eyes had lost their autocratic air. It was like a shell had been cracked, revealing their inner liquid warmth.

She shook her head. "You of all people should know I'm not one of you."

"Do not tell me what I know or don't know." He sat back, his eyes never leaving hers. "You are one of us. What puzzles me is why you refuse to see it."

She shrugged facetiously. "Maybe because my father was English, my mother and grandfather, French. I think that probably explains why I'm not one of your people."

He rose and came closer to her. "You know it is nothing to do with genetics." He took her hand and slapped it against her heart. "It is here where your identity lies, it is here, in your heart, that dictates your nationality, your people, where you belong, your home. And I won't stop until *you* know this, too."

She tugged her hand away and stumbled back. "Why are you torturing me? Why are you doing this? Trying to punish me for rejecting you, hey?" She stepped back further.

He narrowed his eyes and shook his head. "What makes you run from happiness, *habibti*? But why do I ask, when I doubt you know."

"Don't play games with me, Zavian!" she warned, walking quickly toward the door.

"I'm going to do whatever it takes to make you see."

She paused with her hand on the door handle. "What if I don't want to see?"

"You are afraid. That, I had not imagined."

She shook her head and opened the door. "You can play your games if you like, Zavian. But the end result will be the same. You need to marry someone who your countrymen approve of. Without that, you won't have a country."

She slipped out the door without waiting for an answer. She knew where her bags would have been taken and quickly ran up the back stairs to the guest wing, only stopping when she knew she wasn't being followed.

She flung the windows open wide and gulped in the hot, fragrant air. Far overhead, a falcon cried out. She looked up to see the bird call again as it flew past. The light was harsh, the landscape stunning, and she felt her connection to it at a vital level.

She had a vivid recollection of when Zavian's father had offered her the money to leave, a chance to run from commitment, and she'd taken it. At first she'd believed that she was doing it for him and the country. It was only later that she realized that there was something else—something deep-seated within her, a scared child at her center who was terrified of committing to a person who had never spoken of love. From an early age, her grandfather had ingrained on her how love was the only thing to be trusted in this world. Everything else was ephemeral—here one moment, and the next, turned to dust. Only love continued, and there was no substitute, no second best. There hadn't been for him—he'd loved her grandmother until her premature death—and there wouldn't be for her, either.

A shiver ran through her, but it had nothing to do with the breeze that came from the open window. Zavian was right. She *was* afraid. She was scared of falling for Zavian's magnetism again and then being cast adrift after he'd tired of her—either before or after he made an arranged marriage. And she was worth more—her grandfather had shown her that.

CHAPTER 5

Zavian knew her secret now, Gabrielle thought, as she descended the stairs to attend the breakfast she'd been summoned to. There was nothing else he could do other than accept her reasoning. It sounded simple in her head, but as Zavian rose to greet her, alone once more, she knew it would be anything but simple.

"You slept well, I trust?"

She nodded warily. "Yes, thank you."

He indicated she should take the seat opposite him. "Then why do you look so tired?"

She shot him an annoyed look. "No more than you."

He didn't appear perturbed by her response. He'd seemed to have shed his kingship the moment he'd set foot inside the desert castle. "I had things on my mind, as I'm sure did you." He beckoned staff to step forward to serve them breakfast.

As the head steward exchanged a few words with Zavian, Gabrielle looked around. It hadn't changed at all since she was last here. Then there'd been only Zavian and herself, which was just as well as neither of them had any thought for anyone else.

She took a sip of coffee and closed her eyes as the thick, fragrant brew took her back to that time, a few months after she'd returned from completing her degree at Oxford, when she and Zavian had made love for the first time. It had been here, in this castle, in the room in which she was staying. She'd lost her virginity that night to him, as well as her heart. She blushed at the memory of how completely and utterly she'd given of herself and how her surrender had been rewarded with Zavian's generous lovemaking. That was the real reason she hadn't slept. When she opened her eyes again, Zavian was staring at her with an easily-read expression. It was the reason he hadn't slept either.

Her blush deepened as his eyes swept over her face. It took in the delicate shadows which had formed over the nights since she'd been told she had no choice but to face this moment, down to her lips which she instinctively moistened. Only then did he look away.

"I see you aren't eating," he said. "You should." He leaned forward, his eyes hot. "We are leaving this morning."

She put down her coffee cup. "So that was it? We come here to have the truth extracted from me, and now you know what happened, we return to the capital, I complete my contract and return home."

"You appear to have grasped entirely the wrong idea of what is about to happen."

She frowned. "What other outcome is there?"

"What you don't appear to have grasped is that you've told me nothing I didn't know, or at least guess, already." He leaned back in his chair and took a long sip of coffee. "*That* is not the reason for us being here."

"Then why go to all the trouble of leaving your work to bring me here?"

"It was the first step. I needed you to know that I knew."

"Surely there were far easier ways of telling me."

"The telling was not the objective."

She shook her head in confusion. "You're talking in riddles."

He leaned forward, and her senses were filled with him. "This isn't about me telling you anything. This is about you needing to understand."

"I think you underestimate my powers of comprehension. I know you, Zavian. I know how you think, what you like, what you want."

His lips twisted into a disbelieving hint of a smile. "And what is it that you think I want now?"

"You hate that I left you, and you want to reignite our relationship before your impending marriage—which is everywhere in the news—and then drop me when you've had enough and humiliate me in the process."

He shook his head, no trace of a smile now. "For all your education and intelligence, you have no idea how a man's mind works."

"Then enlighten me. Because I'm dying to know."

"We're only here to further your education, to make you understand, not me, not the desert or the country, but yourself. To be clear, and it seems I must be, I've brought you here to understand the truth about yourself."

His explanation hadn't come close to any of the things she'd anticipated he'd say.

"Myself? You want me to know myself? That's a bit arrogant, isn't it? To imagine I don't know myself? Or, as I suspect, because my thoughts don't agree with yours, you intend to change mine, under the guise of 'education'." She sat back and huffed out an unfunny laugh. "Such autocratic arrogance."

He rose. "Possibly, but that doesn't mean to say it's not true." He tossed down his napkin. "Continue, finish your breakfast because you'll need all the energy you can find."

"What now? Have you got me on an assault course to assist me in sorting my muddled thoughts?"

"Something like that. The horses are being readied, and we'll be leaving in an hour."

GABRIELLE HADN'T WANTED to enjoy the horse ride so much. It had been easier to begin with, when she'd been able to keep her anger at the downright arrogance of the man close to her, guiding her feelings. But with each rolling canter of her horse—a sensitive Arab mare who responded to her every movement—she settled into the ride and the landscape. If it weren't for the thud of the horse's hooves vibrating through her body, and the astringent heat of the desert filling her lungs, she'd have thought she was dreaming. Each night of the past twelve months, she'd gone to bed with images of the country she loved so much filling her mind, hoping they'd come to life in her dreams. But this was no dream. A shout from Zavian proved it.

"We'll ride on ahead. Come." He gave his horse free rein, and they galloped off. Her mare could hardly contain herself, and she also charged off and was soon flying to one side, out of the cloud of sand Zavian's horse churned up.

Gabrielle suddenly felt free of the sadness that had dogged her steps ever since a year before when she'd made that fateful decision to leave Zavian. Free of the control that had kept her focused on her work in Oxford, and free of Zavian's control in the palace.

Exhilaration—pure and white-hot—coursed through her veins as they galloped across the desert toward a rocky outcrop in the foothills of the mountains—a place they both knew well.

Finally they slowed, picking their way up and over the

outcrop and descended into the oasis where the Romans had enjoyed the hot spas.

Zavian jumped off his horse and walked around to Gabrielle, and she jumped off into his arms. She stepped away abruptly and looked around the clearing. It was exactly as she remembered it.

"It's just the same," she said in surprise, tethering her horse to a bush. "I thought there were plans to commercialize it."

"Not my plans. My father's. I stopped it."

This made her look at him. "But it could—"

"Have brought in income and been a great tourist attraction? Yes, I know. But some things are sacred and easily damaged. The very things the people would have been coming here to see would have been destroyed."

She walked toward the water, an emerald green under the overhanging palms. In one corner, the fan-like leaves rose and fell on the current of warm air rising from where the hot springs bubbled up, driven by the geothermal activity far below ground.

She sensed Zavian standing behind her.

"Do you remember?" he asked quietly.

Of course she did. How could she not? She nodded. Without meaning to, her gaze shifted to where her grandfather's tents had once stood as they'd excavated in the place where, decades earlier, he'd found the Qur'an. There was nothing there now, of course. But she found what she was looking for, the dark entrance to the cave.

Zavian was about to speak when the sound of vehicles approaching broke through the charged silence, and he sighed and walked off to meet his staff. They were soon following orders, erecting tents for both themselves some distance away, and the main one in the prominent position overlooking the pool, in front of the cave wall. Gabrielle knew from experience that the tent would be connected to the cave and would be an extension of it. She'd slept there after all—before, when she and her grandfather had been working on the site, and then after. When there had been no one except Zavian and herself, and she'd fallen for him physically, just as she had emotionally.

She cleared her throat, trying desperately not to think of those times. They were gone. Whatever Zavian was trying to do, he'd fail because she knew she was doing the best thing. They could have no future, because his country would have no future if they were together. It was as simple—and as complicated—as that.

Soon the formality of the palace had been replaced by the traditional customs of the Bedouin. Food was being prepared, and the camp readied for the night. She smiled as she watched Zavian's people, free of the formal clothes and actions of the palace, sit cross-legged as they prepared the food while listening to one man talk.

She sat, too, and listened to the man who told a story of a journey across the desert. The story emphasized the meaning of family, brotherhood, and belonging to their people. Before she knew it, Zavian had seated himself beside her and joined her in listening to the man's story.

After the story ended and the men relaxed to drink and talk, Zavian leaned back against the palm tree's rough bark. "These stories are old. They should be updated. Life isn't like that anymore."

"But it is. For these people, anyway. And they are the people who matter."

He looked at her thoughtfully. "I have a favor to ask, Gabrielle."

She swallowed. "And what's that?"

"Please, show me what you refused to show me the last time we were here."

"I promised grandfather never to show anyone."

"I know. But the place is well controlled now. No one can ransack this place. It is secure in a way that it never was before."

She bit her lip. On the one hand, she felt terrible betraying her grandfather's confidence. But then she was the last one with the knowledge.

She nodded and looked toward the cave. "It's this way."

He followed behind her, so close that she felt as if she were in orbit, a moon to his earth, earth to his sun, aware of him and the pull of him to her.

She stopped before the cave opening, now half-hidden by the adjoining tent. But, instead of going inside, she walked along a narrow ridge behind it. Zavian followed her.

The undergrowth had grown rampant since she'd last been there. She and her grandfather and a few trusted servants had ensured the path to the site wasn't obvious and that it would re-grow and hide the precious site within months. And it had. Now, years later, it was impossible to imagine that the narrow ledge led anywhere. Certainly, from the frown on Zavian's disbelieving face, he had no idea that what he was about to see existed.

They had to get on their hands and knees and crawl the last little way. When she emerged, her bare arms were scratched from the thorny scrub, but she didn't feel a thing as she jumped down from the ledge onto the tiled surface covered with sand and dust. It was instantly apparent from the lack of footprints that no one had been there in years. It had remained a secret.

Zavian emerged from the bush, equally scratched, and equally uncaring, and stepped into the space beside her. "What the hell?"

She grinned. "That's not a very kingly thing to say."

He strode out into the center of the tiled area and turned

360 degrees, absorbing the towering trees, the cliff face on one side, and the sharp drop down to the plains far below on the far side. Ancient hot pools were carved into the cliff face with steps leading up to them. The remains of columns dotted the enclosure, nearly enveloped in trailing plants, lush under the thermal steam. Rock faces which hid the place from the world bore the traces of paintings, groups around a pool, men and women in various stages of undress. It had been a secret escape from the desert to the abundance of everything. Fruit trees, offspring of long-ago planted fruit, still clung to the rocks, watered far below the surface by underground water. Their vines were thick and ancient, grown into the rock for support, their fruits hanging lush and plumply purple, attracting both animals and birds.

"It's the place of which the ancients used to speak," said Zavian. He turned to face her, his expression serious. "Isn't it, Gabrielle? The Havilah of old when the three kingdoms were one."

She nodded. "It is. Grandfather discovered it but swore all of those who came with him to secrecy. He'd intended to return to finish excavating. But it never happened, and—"

"And those who he'd been with perished in the same accident," continued Zavian.

"Yes."

"Leaving only you." At last, he turned to her, and his gaze settled on her. "Would you ever have revealed its existence, if I hadn't insisted?"

"Honestly? No. I thought it better to remain secret. A part of history. I couldn't bear the thought of it ruined by looting."

"But that might have happened anyway. If I'd known about it, I could have secured it."

She plucked a fruit, brushed it, and bit into it, the juice dribbling down her chin. "Maybe, maybe not. I decided to leave it alone and let it take its chances without me."

"And are you not fearful of what I might do?"

She shook her head. She should have been, but she wasn't anymore. She didn't know why. "No, it's time, and it's only right."

He reached out his hand, and she took it. Again, it felt right.

"So this was where my forebears came for sensual pleasure. The rumors and legends were correct. It *is* a fitting place. No wonder it has gained such a reputation."

The air, redolent with abundance and sensuality, seemed to enter her pores. "Yes, a strange place to find the Khasham Qur'an."

"So, are you going to show me?"

"The place where my grandfather found the Qur'an?"

His eyes nodded.

"Of course. This way."

She led him through a narrow gap, past another pool fringed with palm trees, out to a part of the desert far from the nomad's tracks, where there was nothing, at least to most people's eyes. But Gabrielle knew each and every contour of this land. She could walk it in her sleep and often had done.

The sun was beginning to set by the time they'd made their way to the site of the original dig, now covered by a decade of sands, which had shifted and peaked and obliterated any trace of excavation.

Gabrielle stopped and looked across at the craggy hillside above the secret oasis, then at another oasis, which shimmered in the distance. She walked a few more paces forward and then retrieved her compass from her pocket to make sure. She nodded in satisfaction and dropped to her knees. She patted the ground. "Here."

She lifted the sand in the palm of her hand and let it sift through her fingers, the lowering sun turning the sands orange, a sharp contrast to the dark blue sky. She suddenly realized Zavian hadn't moved.

He stood rooted to the spot looking down at her, and then at the ground before her, and then around at its setting. He shook his head. "I never imagined it would be here." He pointed to the oasis. "Our people pass through that oasis on their way to the mountains."

"Unaware that this ever existed, apart from the songs and poems," she added.

"Which describe it as it was, but not where it is."

He dropped down beside her, squinting into the lowering sun.

"So," he said. "What is the story which you will write to go with the Khasham Qur'an?"

"I'll write of how it was created long ago when this land was at the heart of the world's economy and learning and religion. I'll write of how the inks were ground from pigment brought from far and near, of how the parchment was made, and of how wondrous the palace and buildings were which once stood here."

"The fabled land of Havilah, indeed," murmured Zavian. "And what else will you write?"

"Of how the Qur'an passed from hand to hand. Of how both its beauty and its contents bound these communities, making sense of their world."

"But that's not enough."

She looked at him sharply.

"I want the personal. That's what touches people."

"I can't do that."

"Try."

She swallowed and looked straight ahead at the dying sun, now strangely swollen, its colors muted into eerie tones of burnt umber. "When my grandfather showed it to me"—she looked at him with an embarrassed smile—"I told him my tears were because of the sun. But they weren't."

"That's better."

"I'll write of *how* it was found." She needed to be precise.

"But not where."

"No, not where."

She refused to look at him because she felt the effect of his proximity already. "He shouldn't have done it. It was against all his professional ethics, to cover up his tracks."

"He left a myth surrounding it, instead of the facts."

"The facts would have destroyed this place. Taken its soul away." She couldn't resist. She looked at him. "That's what he believed anyway."

His eyes narrowed with curiosity. "And is that what you believe? That places have souls?"

She nodded briefly, her eyes straying to his lips before returning to his eyes, which revealed an even more intense curiosity. He lifted a lock of her hair which had fallen across her face and tucked it behind her ear, stroking the length of it briefly before dropping his hand once more. "I know that's a strange thing to believe," she said softly.

He shrugged. "Many people in this world believe many things, and who am I to judge whether they are strange?"

She smiled. "You sound almost humble."

"You mistake strength and purpose for arrogance." He inclined his head closer to hers, and she gave a sharp intake of breath, which brought his scent into her lungs. "Don't confuse things, Gabrielle. I'm a man who knows what he wants, and I intend to get it."

She swallowed with a sudden stab of fear. "And how exactly do you intend to do that?"

A smile flickered on his lips, the first she'd seen in a long time. "Through something you once showed me... subtlety."

He leaned closer, lifted her chin with his finger, and

kissed her gently on the lips. He'd withdrawn before she could react. The kiss had been fleeting, but the effects were far from it. It brought something to life deep inside, something she didn't want.

She jumped up and stepped away from him, pushing the back of her hand against her mouth as if to wipe the kiss away. She shook her head. "You shouldn't have done that."

He was beside her in an instant, taking her hand. "Don't tell me that you don't want my touch, that you don't imagine the feel of my lips upon yours, because I don't believe you."

"It might be true, but it doesn't mean that I'm going to act on it."

She tried to tug her hand away, but he kissed it, holding it to his face and closing his eyes. "Gabrielle, I know why you're resisting me. It's because you feel you don't belong, but you do. You talked of this land having a soul. No one who was not a part of this land would sense such a thing."

"I know what you're saying, Zavian, but it doesn't matter. What people believe is what matters."

"Which is why the stories are so important. We have to make them see. But before that, I have to make *you* see."

"And how do you intend to do that?"

"To make you *feel* again."

He tugged her to him, and she couldn't stop herself. He caressed her shoulders, holding her close to him, searching her face, as if for signs of resistance. There were none. Her power to stop the inevitable was blown. And then his lips were upon hers, but the kiss was no tender glancing meeting of the lips. This time his mouth was hungry for passion, searching out her tongue until her stomach flipped with desire. He drew her closer to him, and she could feel every inch of tension, every contour of muscle, and his increasing arousal.

Her blood raced with desire, her sex was wet with it as

she pushed herself against him. His heartbeat exploded under the palm of her hand, which had somehow slipped beneath his shirt. She wanted him as she'd never wanted him before—with a raw passion which bypassed any thinking or feeling. She simply needed him.

He pulled away first and pressed his forehead against hers. Their breathing came in jagged pants as desire—hot and intense—gripped them both.

"I could have you here, now, Gabrielle."

"Then do it." She caressed his hips, urging him with another kiss to surrender to the lust she knew he felt.

But he pulled away again, brushing his thumb against her swollen bottom lip. "No, *habibti*." He turned his head to one side, looking out over the horizon. "Look."

And she did. But what she saw wasn't what she'd expected to see. The sky was dark, but not a natural dark, it was bruised with the rising cloud of sand as it swirled in winds which they had yet to feel the full strength of.

"*Khamseen...*" she said.

He nodded. "We must go now."

He took her hand, and they ran back toward the trees, the wind suddenly coming upon them, lifting the palms up and down, as if urging them to move faster. The wind tugged at their clothes, swirled her hair around her face, plastering it against her cheeks and eyes until she couldn't see anymore. She could only follow his lead, only respond to the grip of his hand over hers as they ran for their lives.

CHAPTER 6

*T*he rising winds shrieked through the branches of the trees as if they'd been roused by the devil. The giant palm fronds, usually so stately, rose and fell with force, slapping against Gabrielle's arm as she sheltered from their blows.

Zavian went ahead, pushing the branches and leaves aside for her, his other arm around her shoulders as if worried she'd be blown away.

Eventually, they emerged to find his people in a state of panic, searching for them. There was chaos all around as the tents were quickly taken down and packed away. Zavian and Gabrielle were ushered into the main cave, and the doors slammed on them. While the others sought shelter in the network of caves, Zavian stuffed the gaps around the ancient wooden door to prevent the sand from filtering through. Together they passed along the passage and into the main area.

Gabrielle had been in other caves but never this one. This was reserved for the royal family. And, as she looked around, she realized that it had been prepared recently for her.

She turned to Zavian. "You planned this."

He walked to the torches placed around the walls in sconces and lit them. One by one, the flickering light grew, illuminating the bed which took up half the space, and the seating and dining areas which took up the other half. Everything was fresh, everything readied for use. There was fresh water flowing into the tap from the hillside, as well as bottled water. Off to one side, in a cold store, was food and wine, enough to see them safely through a week if necessary. They had everything they needed.

He glanced at her while he lit the final light. "Yes, of course."

Anger filled her veins, replacing the lust which had ignited only minutes before. "How dare you? You play me like a toy, forcing me to come here to be with you, trapping me in your palace, to ensure you get what you want."

He didn't reply. Instead, he poured some water and dunked his face and head into it, ridding himself of the sand. He tossed his head back, and water spattered onto the floor and across to her. He pushed his fingers through his hair and wiped his face dry before turning to her.

"I'd do the same if I were you. Otherwise, the sand will irritate your eyes."

"I don't need the sand! You're enough to irritate me!"

"I'm sure," he replied calmly. "But I'd still wash your face. Your eyes are red."

"That's because you're driving me crazy!" she said as she poured water into the bowl to relieve her stinging eyes. She patted her face dry. "You planned everything. How could you, Zavian?"

He sat down and stretched an arm along the back of the sofa. "I know you consider me to be all-powerful, but believe me, I cannot control the desert *khamseen*."

She narrowed her eyes in response. "No, but you must

have known it was forecast, and yet you decided to make the trip out here anyway."

He shrugged. "That sounds irresponsible. Do you really consider I would do such a thing?"

"It *is* irresponsible, and I'm sure Naseer won't be impressed. Your country must come first, always."

The upward tilt of his lips dropped suddenly. "Believe me, it does."

Her anger was halted by the seriousness of his expression, which she didn't understand. "You're a contradiction," she said. "A manipulative, controlling contradiction."

"I'm not sure you're allowed to insult your king," he replied mildly.

She grunted and twisted her hair off her face, looping it onto itself. "You're not a king here, now, with me."

His eyes darkened. He rose, and her heart stopped as he walked past her and opened a bottle of wine. He poured two glasses and returned to her.

"There's food, too, if you're hungry."

She shook her head and accepted a glass of wine. "Wine? That's not usual outside the palace, surely?"

"Not in traditional gatherings, but you know that our country is a mixture of the west and east. We manage it by using our discretion."

"And I guess there's nowhere quite as discrete as being in a cave while the desert wind whips up the sand all around us, making it impossible for us to exit, or for others to enter."

"Exactly." He took another sip and let out a long sigh, his eyes grazing over her. "Now, where were we?"

She shook her head. She didn't want to remind him, but by the look on his face, he didn't need reminding.

"You know I thought it would be different, kissing you. But it wasn't. It was as if the intervening time had evaporated

—disappeared—and it was only yesterday that we were together."

She *had* to resist. This whole set up had been to seduce her, but she didn't want that, did she? "Maybe, but that's irrelevant."

He smiled, and her eyes slid to his lips as inappropriate thoughts blasted into her mind.

A silence descended as he looked thoughtful. "Tell me, Gabrielle. What is it you want?"

She nearly choked on her sip of wine. "You ask me what I want? I thought this was all about what *you* wanted."

"I repeat, what is it you want?"

"I want to be... free," she said simply, from between dry lips, the words wrenched from her.

"Free of what?"

She looked up and caught his gaze. "Free of feeling things I don't want to feel."

He sat forward, his face more intense if anything. "There, you see, we both want the same things. The only difference between you and me is that I want to free myself of this obsession by indulging it."

She shook her head instinctively. "No, that's not the way. Only by absence, by depriving ourselves of what we had, can we recover."

"Recover," he grunted. "You make it sound like a disease."

"I think it is. It's certainly the opposite of ease."

He nodded. "And how do you treat a disease? With a small amount of it, until the body moderates its response."

She opened her mouth to speak but was unable to contradict him. It was science. And it was science that she believed in, wasn't it?

"You think a little more passion will ease the need?" she asked tentatively.

"I'm counting on it."

"It's been the same for you, too, then?"

"It gets worse over time, my need for you."

"And you don't want it," she ventured.

"No." It was a brief answer, but it was all she needed.

She closed her eyes and nodded. She turned away, not wanting to witness the raw need in his eyes, which reflected her own. She jumped up and rubbed her arms. He followed her.

"Are you cold?"

She shook her head, not trusting her voice.

"Then what is the matter?"

When she looked into his eyes, she saw the shock as he registered her tears. "The matter is that I want you to hold me. The matter is that I've never stopped wanting that, not a day since I left you."

His kiss robbed her of the need to speak any further. He felt... like bliss, she realized as her mind lifted. Her thoughts and fears simply evaporated under the magical caress of his lips against hers, teasing her lips apart. As his tongue explored hers, ratcheting up the response elsewhere in her body, she breathed him in. He tasted of wine and sand; he tasted of everything she'd been needing since she'd left him.

She moaned as his hands cupped her face and held her steady. As he continued to explore her mouth, his intense focus was on that kiss, of what he was giving her and of what he was finding in her. She didn't know what that was, but she knew she wanted more of it. Her heartbeat pounded, and she thought that he must hear it, that it filled the intense quiet of the cave, the noise outside deadened by the thick walls.

Her fingers splayed around his hips, shifting until they reached his muscled stomach. But with each new sensation of her fingers against his skin, she wanted more. She tilted her head back and opened her mouth, allowing his tongue to mimic what she wanted elsewhere. Her thoughts had moved from the kiss to sex in the split second his lips had touched hers, and it seemed he knew. Because he drew away and held her face firmly in his, his thumbs sweeping over her cheeks.

She leaned closer to him, to capture those lips once more, but he stood back and slipped off his jacket. He paused as he dropped it on the chair.

She followed his lead and pulled off her abaya. Then she unbuttoned her shirt. His eyes followed her fingers, lingering on her breasts as she drew back the fabric and slid it off her shoulders and tossed it onto the chair, alongside his jacket.

She stood only in her bra and jeans. She inhaled sharply before continuing to undress. She had no intention of waiting for him to take off the rest of his clothes. She wanted to show him what she felt, and there seemed no better way.

Within seconds she stood naked in front of him. His throat convulsed, and then he tore off his shirt. He stepped toward her and kissed each breast in turn before dropping to his knees. He pressed a kiss against her naked stomach, his eyes closing as he trailed kisses further along her stomach, his hands caressing her behind as his mouth lowered. She gasped, gripping his head with her hands as his tongue found another target.

She thanked God for his ability to focus with steely strength, as his complete attention was given to tasting her as if she were all he wanted in this desert. He wasn't only intent on giving her pleasure, but she could sense how much he was enjoying it, too. It was in the way his tongue explored her, and his eyes closed as he focused entirely on her, his hands moving around her bottom and her sex, turning her legs to jelly and her heart into overdrive.

With each lap of his tongue, each slide of his fingers around and inside her, the coiling tension inside her tightened. She dug her fingers into his hair, terrified he'd stop. But he did the opposite, escalating his ministrations until she couldn't stop herself, but called out his name as she pulsed around his finger.

He continued to hold her steady as her limbs trembled, and licked her arousal, tasting it as if it were the most costly, desired wine that he could have asked for. Then he rose and, without a word, slid one hand under her, the other around her shoulders, and carried her to the bed.

There, he laid her gently on the silk coverlet, richly printed with bold geometric Bedouin designs. As he finished undressing, she watched him, just as he'd watched her.

Zavian was impressive when he was dressed, but without clothes, he was awesome. His powerful body was no longer hidden behind the trappings of royalty. The strong lines of his bones and muscles, honed by years of sport and riding in the desert, revealed his innate power. She reached out to touch him.

As her fingers made contact with that part of him she craved, he closed his eyes and breathed in sharply. The sudden awareness of her power over him made her bold. She stroked up his length before circling and caressing its base. Then she rose and went on tiptoe and kissed him, feeling his erection pressing against her.

All it took was for her to raise a thigh and rub it down his hip for him to groan and swiftly lift her until she had both legs around his hips. He took a few steps until her back was pressed against the lush velvet of a wall hanging. She tilted her hips, and he entered her with one long thrust.

He held her there for a long moment, pinned against the tapestry, speared by his erection as if she were a butterfly and he were the pin. He held her in place so he could admire her beauty, and revel in his sense of possession of her—a sense of possession which she knew she'd never be able to give him in any other way. But here, naked, making love, she wanted to give him everything it was in her power to give.

He rolled his forehead against hers, kissing her nose, her cheek, nose again, lips, and then her neck, nuzzling her with kisses and nips until it was she in the end who moved first, lifting herself off him, desperate for another thrust.

It was as if he was awakened. He drew away from her, his eyes narrowed and dark as he took her, thrusting into her with a regularity with which she couldn't argue. It took her to the place of annihilation where she was not herself, she was more—she was someone who existed only in relation to him, someone who needed him to take her to the place of no thought, only pleasure.

It was only after the blast of shocking sensation shot through her body—causing her muscles to flex around him, milking him for what she needed from him—that he allowed himself the same release. His buttocks tensed, and he thrust into her with short sharp thrusts, his eyes narrowed to slits of obsidian. When he closed them, the spell broke.

He allowed her legs to slide through his hands and fall, quivering, to the floor. Together they fell to the bed, her sex sensitive and wet as his seed leaked down her thighs. She touched it, and his gaze followed her as she brought her sperm-soaked fingers to her clitoris and made herself jerk as her sensitive bud responded to the stimulation. Gone was the shy, demure academic. Zavian had unleashed a wildness in her, matched by his own essential nature.

He entered her slowly this time, making sure she felt every inch of him against her sensitive skin, as he penetrated her. She tilted her head back, and he kissed her neck and lower, as they found a new rhythm, slow and languorous, sensuous and captivating.

"Gabrielle." He mussed her hair with his lips.

She softly grunted as no thought, no response, came to mind.

"Gabrielle," he repeated more urgently, as he lifted

himself from her and began to increase the rhythm, to awake her from her stupor of sensation. She kissed him, and the kiss continued as he thrust into her until they came together, crying out, their mouths against each other.

Finally, their breathing subsided, and their bodies came to rest. The cave was filled with only the faintest movement of wind from the storm outside. Inside the candles' flames rose perfect, undisturbed by any breeze. There was only their heartbeats and breathing growing more regular as Gabrielle drifted off to sleep, lulled from thought or recriminations by the total relaxation of her body and mind, as well as the touch of Zavian's fingers over her body—caressing, marveling and worshipping all at the same time.

ZAVIAN CONTINUED to trace his fingers over Gabrielle's sleeping body. She was beautiful; he'd remembered that. She was tender and yielding to his touch, completely in tune with his body and mind; he remembered that also. What he hadn't remembered was how she made him feel. It was as if he forgot himself when he was with her. That together, they were more important than either one of them. It was a loss, but there was no doubt that it wasn't lack which now filled his veins, but a deep sense of peace. He felt "right" for the first time since she'd left him. And at that moment, he realized that making love to her wouldn't cure anything. It merely showed him how much he needed her, to be the person he wished to be. Without her, he was nothing.

As he gentled his hand on the small of her back she shifted a little and lifted her face to his. He brushed a kiss across her lips and settled back, his other hand under his head.

The wild night raged all around them, scarcely touching them within the womb of the mountain, which held them safe and secure. He closed his eyes as the last of the candles sputtered out, leaving complete darkness.

No, what making love had made him realize was that he needed to adjust his plans. There would be no future without Gabrielle. He just needed to make her see. And he would.

A smile flickered over his lips as he drifted off to sleep.

A REPETITIVE THUD AWAKENED GABRIELLE. She sat up suddenly, wondering where she was in the semi-darkness. But a hand on her back restricted her movement. She pushed her hair out of her eyes and looked around.

Zavian's arm lay over her protectively. He opened his eyes and smiled at her with a warmth which made her stomach flutter. He pulled her to him until she rolled on top of him, and she could feel he was fully awake.

"Where do you think you're going?" he asked, pushing away her hair.

They were interrupted by another pummeling at the door.

She raised her eyebrows. "Not me. You. I doubt it's me they want." Shouts followed another bout of pummeling. "It's you. And unless you go now"—she glanced down at his arousal—"we'll be delaying them quite some time."

He kissed her, sighed and rolled on top of her, hesitated a moment, and then leaped up. He pulled on his trousers, pushed his fingers through his hair, and went out to the corridor and opened the door.

Gabrielle pulled on a robe and retreated to a corner where she couldn't be seen, listening while his men talked to him in an undertone.

By the time Zavian returned, Gabrielle had dressed and done the best she could with her hair. She grimaced at herself in the mirror. A bath would have to wait until she could leave the cave and use the tent's luxurious facilities.

Zavian returned and closed the door behind him. "We must return to the city."

"What's happened?" asked Gabrielle with a frown.

"Something has come up which I need to attend to urgently."

She couldn't prevent a sly smile. "So your plans are thwarted. It's not just going to be you and me, out in the desert."

But he didn't smile back. "My plans have changed, Gabrielle. You, me, last night… it has changed everything."

She pressed her lips together. She'd believed him when he said they would take what they desired and be able to leave. Not for her, but she'd believed that he would indeed have sated his desire for her.

"It changes nothing, Zavian. Everything is exactly as it was twenty-four hours earlier. Nothing has changed," she repeated, her voice low and urgent.

He smoothed his hands over her shoulders, and held her firmly, as if to drive the seriousness of his message through his fingertips into her body. "I thought that by making love to you, I would rid myself of my obsession. But it's proved the opposite. I want you, Gabrielle. Not just for now, not just for tonight but for tomorrow and always."

"It cannot be."

"It has to be. I will show you that this world is yours, as well as mine."

All she could do was shake her head. He might believe it, but she could not.

CHAPTER 7

*T*he return trip was made in silence. It was like a wall had slammed between them. Zavian drove, his eyes fixed on the road in front, his mind miles away. Gabrielle felt his distance all the more acutely after such intimacy.

It was only when they stopped upon entering the palace compound and he switched the engine off, that they both turned to see the helicopter readying itself for takeoff.

She looked back at him. "You're going somewhere?" She shook her head, bewildered. "What's happened?"

"Naseer wishes to discuss something of urgency, but after that I'll be leaving. I won't be gone long."

"But—" She stopped herself. He was king and could come and go as he wished. He'd had a night of sex with her and now couldn't wait to leave her, even after what he'd said about wanting her for always.

"But nothing. I will explain later after I return." As he glanced out at the waiting helicopter, the palms moving madly under the breeze from the blades, his face was grim.

"Right." She stepped out the car and into the fierce sun,

the heat magnified as it bounced off the buildings. "Right," she muttered, this time to herself, as she watched Naseer exchange a few brief, urgent words with Zavian, before Naseer shot her a dark look and returned inside.

King Zavian bin Ameen Al Rasheed—for that was what he'd instantly become from the moment he'd left their bedroom—stepped inside the helicopter, and it took off into the brilliant blue sky. What the hell was going on?

～

"So," said Sheikh Amir al-Rahman, King of Janub Havilah, his hands clasped in front of him, his face grim. "Our countries have twice had to be on alert to repel the invaders from Jazira. The second time there was a fatality. Luckily it was theirs, but unless we get this pact with Tawazun signed and sealed, we can look forward to more of the same. And this time, our people may not escape so lightly."

King Roshan of Sharq Havilah entered the room, took a swig of his coffee, and slid into his seat. "Apologies," he said. "I was delayed."

Zavian rolled his eyes. "Who was she?"

Roshan grinned. "I couldn't possibly divulge the name of the lady in question. I have her reputation to consider."

"I think her reputation must have been the last thing on her mind if she decided to get together with you!" pointed out Amir.

Both Amir and Roshan laughed, but Zavian didn't.

Amir noticed, and his face suddenly stilled and looked thoughtful. "You called the meeting, Zavian. What is so important that you want us to meet, not two weeks since our last meeting?"

Zavian looked first from Amir to Roshan and then back to Amir, trying to find the words he'd rehearsed in the helicopter ride from his city to here, their meeting place in the desert. But they eluded him still. How could he make sense of the emotion that had blasted into him with all the force of the *khamseen*, obliterating all traces of what had gone before, since his night with Gabrielle?

Roshan pulled a face and shifted in his seat, casting a knowing glance at Amir. "Oh dear," he said, with his characteristic insouciance, "This sounds serious."

Amir grunted but didn't move his gaze from Zavian. Zavian returned it in full measure. Once, as boys, they'd been fiercely competitive, but they were now close, and would take a bullet for each other. The underlying strength of their relationship remained intact.

"It is serious," said Zavian. "I can no longer pursue marriage to the Sheikha of Tawazun."

Amir didn't blink, but Roshan groaned and let his head fall back against the chair. He opened his eyes slowly and stared at the dark ancient beams that intersected the whitewashed plaster ceiling.

"Why?" asked Amir.

All three men had agreed to leave niceties at the door when they met, in favor of straight-talking. They'd reckoned they needed to cut to the chase with each other when there was little possibility of receiving honest, unbiased advice from anyone else. But, even so, Amir's directness rankled.

"Because my plans have changed."

Roshan jumped out of his seat and raked his fingers through his hair, twisting around to glance at them both. "He's fallen in love."

Amir frowned. "Zavian?" he said in a voice that doubted Roshan's assertion. "Is Roshan correct?"

Zavian gripped his hands into fists and noted they were sweaty. He couldn't remember the last time he'd been afraid. Or, rather, he could. The day he realized Gabrielle had no intention of returning. He could sit through councils of war, he could stay calm in any crisis it seemed, other than ones of the heart. That, he thought, was the issue. He didn't want to have a heart.

"Roshan is interpreting facts as they would pertain to him."

Roshan shook his head in mock despair and came and sat at the other end of the table. "I'm stating facts, Zavian, just as we've always agreed to."

"I've not fallen in love; I'm not in love." He waved his hand in dismissal at the foolish notions. "These are romantic figments of your imagination, Roshan."

Roshan grunted. "Mine and the rest of the world. Except you, apparently."

"I repeat, love does not come into this. Is that statement enough for you?"

Roshan shrugged but didn't look convinced.

Amir held out a hand to stop the argument. "Whether you are, or are not, is of no importance here. What is, is what plans have changed, and how they will impact us."

Zavian nodded and rubbed his still balled fist against his lips briefly, before resting his hands on the table and eyeing first Amir and then Roshan. "The marriage cannot proceed."

"I see," said Amir.

Roshan's face assumed a look of thunder, but he didn't speak.

"And you are certain of this?"

Zavian nodded. "I am." He licked his dry lips. "I wish to marry another."

"I knew it!" exploded Roshan.

"This has nothing to do with love. She is simply…" He hesitated as he struggled to find the right word to describe her. "Simply the person who…" He sighed. "Who," he repeated, hoping he'd find the words before his sentence ended, "I need…" He was still groping for the right word before he suddenly realized further words were superfluous. He'd stated the situation exactly as it was. He needed Gabrielle. He needed no one else.

"You need," repeated Roshan sarcastically. "Whatever you call it, you're off the market, and so it falls to me." He swore under his breath.

"I can hardly remonstrate when I, myself, have done the same thing," said Amir. "Roshan? What do you think?"

"What do I think?" he said with bitter emphasis. He shook his head and sighed. "I think that you have both lost your minds. That you have both put your personal happiness ahead of our three countries which comprise this land of ours." He rose and gripped the table, his tall frame looming over them both. "I think that it is as well that I, with all my reputation as a womanizer, set the least store by love. Because, Zavian, whatever you wish to call your requirement to wed this, whoever she is, don't fool yourself it isn't love." He sucked in a deep breath and pushed himself off the table. "Luckily for us all, I am immune to such feelings. I adore women—plural—but fortunately, I don't love any particular one of them. The Sheikha of Tawazun will be as good as any to be my wife."

Zavian hadn't realized until that moment how afraid he'd been that Roshan would refuse, as he had every right to. Zavian had volunteered to marry the Tawazun sheikha to ensure ongoing peace for their worlds, and he was now reneging on the deal. With Amir also married, that left only Roshan to do the deed.

"Thank you, Roshan. And I am sorry it has come to this, but there is nothing I can do about it."

Roshan looked from Amir to Zavian and shook his head in mock despair. "For all your alpha male machismo, you two are like putty in a woman's hand."

Zavian and Amir exchanged insulted looks, but both their responses were brought to an abrupt halt when Roshan muttered an oath. "Luckily for us all, while I might look like pretty putty on the outside, my strength is a steel heart. I know how to have fun, and I know how to keep myself safe." He looked from one to the other. "Leave it with me."

They all rose and shook hands, but it was Roshan who left first.

Zavian and Amir watched Roshan jump into the waiting helicopter and turn east into the bright blue sky.

Zavian was both relieved that his way was now clear and concerned about the pressure which was now sitting on Roshan's shoulders.

"It's down to him now," said Amir, his eyes watching the dwindling dot in the sky, the hum growing ever fainter. He looked at Zavian. "I hope he's right."

"In what?"

"That the link we thought to be the weakest in our armor will turn out to be the strongest."

IT HADN'T TAKEN LONG for Gabrielle to convert her words around the story of the Khasham Qur'an into a multi-media presentation that could be used online and in the museum itself. Despite pressure from the director, she refused to front the video. She felt that job should go to a citizen of Gharb Havilah—not a foreigner like her. However, she didn't mind describing to camera how the Qur'an had been found and her grandfather's part in it. She'd omitted the exact location of the find. From there, she'd described what had followed—the theft of the piece and its ultimate surfacing, years later, in a London auction house. She'd also omitted her part in its repatriation. The story appeared complete. Only she and one other person knew it wasn't.

She turned and smiled at the team as the lights went on. "You've done a fabulous job!"

"We had great material," commented the museum director, rising from his chair. "But Gabrielle is right. Well done, everyone. It's been a long day, and we haven't stopped, so take a break. And as soon as we receive official approval, you can all go home."

Gabrielle walked up to the piece itself, in pride of place, and then looked up at the screen where her passion for the piece had been captured and overlaid with the images of the land and peoples from whence it had come. "They edited it so well," she said to the director, who came to stand beside her.

"They're the best, and work hard. And you haven't stopped either. You should take a break, too."

"I'm fine." Then she looked up and suddenly realized the director also needed to take a break. "But you go. You haven't stopped either."

"I will. But there's one thing I need to know. When will His Majesty approve this display?"

She frowned but didn't look at him directly. "You need his approval?"

"Yes. The instructions are clear. But I'm not receiving a direct answer from his office. I need to know when he'll approve it. No one seems to know where he is. Do you?"

She bit her lip and turned to face the director. He knew. He must have heard that she'd spent the night together, or at the very least, that there was some link between them. "No. I'm afraid I don't know where he is or when he will approve it."

He nodded. "Okay. I'll have my team stay around for the

evening. Hopefully, we'll hear something soon. We'll talk later."

Gabrielle followed him outside and waited while he secured the room. Together they walked back to the main public area of the palace where they would go their separate ways—Gabrielle to the private wing of the palace, and the director to the public, where he and his team were staying while they worked there.

"Look, I'm sorry I can't help." She hesitated as she tried to figure out a way of saying that she'd do what she could, without admitting to any close relationship. "But if I hear anything about, or from, the king, I'll be sure to let you know. And," she relented, "if I see him, I'll be sure to ask him to approve it as soon as possible."

She turned as the blush threatened to give her relationship away and walked without turning back toward the guarded entrance. Even her staying here betrayed that she was someone special. But what the director didn't know was that he wasn't the only one puzzled. As she walked through and the door clanged shut, and an automatic bolt slid into place, she thought she also had no idea what she was to the king anymore.

APART FROM A BRIEF online meeting with the museum staff, where it was confirmed that everyone would have to stay in the palace another night until the exhibit was approved, Gabrielle spent the rest of the evening alone in her room.

She was killing time, she knew. First, she'd had a bath, then checked her social media, not that it was very social. She opened a novel on her e-reader, which she'd been meaning to read for months. She managed two pages before tossing the tablet onto the bed. Her own life was too much like a novel for the ebook to provide an escape.

Instead, she undressed, slipped on a gown, and sat in the easy chair in front of the open French windows, which looked out over the gardens. The scent of mimosa and lemons rose on the cooler night air. She breathed deeply of it and closed her eyes. It smelled of heaven. She rose and stepped onto the paved area immediately outside her window. She was drawn further by the scents and sounds of the night, so calming after a day of bright lights, technology and intense thought.

She opened the wrought-iron gate, which led to the wilder part of the garden. It was only when she'd walked through the palms and bushes toward the central fountain that she stopped. She dipped her hand in the water, which sparkled under the rising crescent moon. Gabrielle allowed the sound of water, the smell of the newly watered gardens, and the heavy scents of flowers to calm her spirits. And it worked until she inhaled another scent.

She opened her eyes wide and turned as the smell of sandalwood, leather, and fresh desert air invaded her nostrils. He was walking toward her. She turned quickly, looking for a place to hide, but it was too late. His eyes were locked on her.

"Gabrielle," Zavian greeted, coming to a stop a few paces away from her.

"Zavian." She nodded awkwardly, instantly forgetting all the doubts and irritation and anger that had filled her day. He was here, now, and she couldn't take her eyes off him. He had the lights of the building behind him, and she couldn't see his face. The silence lengthened between them. "You've been away," she said, trying to fill the silence and instantly regretting it. She sounded as if she'd missed him. But wasn't that the truth?

"Yes. But I'm back now." He paused. "Would you care to join me for a drink?"

95

Her heart thumped. Was he going to continue where they left off in the desert? Or was he going to tell her that he'd had a change of heart and that it had been a one-off, and that there would be no recurrence—that the 'cure' had been affected?

"Sure." She gave him a brief, uncertain smile. She suddenly remembered her promise to the museum director. "We've finished the piece on the Qur'an. We just need your sign-off."

He stepped aside and indicated she should join him. "We'll talk of it over a drink."

He was stalling. Something had happened, but she didn't know what. Was it the Qur'an, was it politics with the kings, or was it her?

He seemed distracted as they walked the short distance across the garden. He opened the gate for her and followed her through. From there, instead of turning to her bedroom suite, they turned the other way, and she found herself stepping into his private apartments. She hadn't realized that they were so close to hers.

At least he didn't show her into his bedroom. Although she wasn't sure if that was a good or bad sign. How could she know what a good sign was when she didn't know what it was she wanted?

"Please take a seat."

He opened the drinks cabinet. "Would you like a drink? An aperitif, maybe?"

She raised an eyebrow. "A gin and tonic would be great, thanks. But I thought you left things like that to the staff. Have you given everyone the night off?"

He glanced at her sideways but ignored her teasing comment, and dropped some ice into a cut-glass tumbler, followed by the gin and tonic, and poured himself a whiskey on ice. He handed her the drink and took a long sip himself before placing it on the table.

"You look like you needed that." She tried to sound as calm as possible, but inside she was anything but.

He shrugged and sat down, his eyes settling on her as if he was trying to decide something.

She took a sip of her drink and pushed it onto the table, sitting up tall. "What's going on, Zavian? You've been behaving strangely ever since we left the cave."

His eyes flickered at the memory, and his expression warmed. "Yes," he agreed.

"Is that it?" She gave a half-laugh.

He sat back in the chair, hooking a leg over his knee as if he didn't have a care in the world. "I met with Amir and Roshan."

"Ah, I remember you used to talk about them. But that was in days before you became king."

"Yes, we were friends first, and now we work together for the good of our kingdoms. We meet regularly, but today's meeting was unscheduled."

"Oh."

An unscheduled meeting. Something extraordinary must have come up. Gabrielle wondered what it might be. There was a pause while she waited for him to elaborate. He didn't.

"So what have you been doing today?" he asked as if the previous conversation hadn't ended on a cliffhanger. "So, you've finished…"

She took another sip of her drink and crossed her legs primly. If he wanted to play it that way, it was fine with her. "Yes. We spent all day on it." She'd intended to give him only the minimum. Still, after she began talking about how the team had worked to produce such an exciting exhibit, she found she'd told him every little detail of how the afternoon had gone. Even at the end of that, she still had no idea what he was thinking. He continued to sit, his hands rubbing his lips from time to time, as if deep in thought, his eyes never leaving hers. "So, are you pleased with the progress of the story?"

He looked up and eyed her straight. "Up to a point."

"And that point is?"

"When you said that you wouldn't front the video because it's not appropriate. Why do you consider it inappropriate?"

She shook her head in disbelief. "Because... I'm not from here." She opened her hands wide. "It's obvious."

"Not to me, it's not."

"But how can I, a European, born in France, raised in England—"

"Only until you were five when you moved to Havilah to be with your grandfather—"

"Sure, only until I was five. But even so, that hardly makes me a native of your country."

"It does in my book. Your heart and soul are pure Havilahi, and until you can see that, your work isn't finished."

She sat back, unable to believe what she was hearing. "What do you mean, it's not finished?"

He finished his whiskey. "Exactly that. It's not finished."

"Do you mean you won't sign it off?"

"That's exactly what I mean."

"But, Zavian," she said in a low voice, deliberately speaking his first name, trying to grab his attention. "It *is* finished. If you don't sign it off, none of the team can go back to their other work."

He shrugged. "Then you'd better hurry up then, hadn't you?" He rose. "The bottom line is that what you've done isn't enough. Not by a long chalk. You still don't understand."

"I understand full well. What I don't do is agree with you."

"It's the same thing." He shrugged.

"Let me get this straight. You want me to change my mind about whether I fit into this country or not?"

"Exactly. I'm glad you understand. It makes it easier."

"Easier? What the hell are you talking about?"

"Tomorrow, you will be joining me at dinner in honor of Sheikh Mohammed."

She shook her head. She knew the old sheikh from old but not in any official capacity. "But why? What role do I have? Surely that's official business?"

"It is. And as to the role? You'll be accompanying me as my consort."

She spluttered, unable to get any word out.

He smiled. "Perhaps I forgot to mention to you about the reason for my meeting with the kings. I told them that the forthcoming marriage negotiations are off."

She frowned. "You're not getting married anymore. But I thought—"

"You thought that my engagement would be announced at the bi-millennial celebration? Yes, that was the original plan. But it's all changed now."

She swallowed drily. "In what way?"

"In the way that Roshan, King of Sharq Havilah, will now progress negotiations to marry Tawazun's sheikha."

"Why? But surely nothing has changed?" The answer throbbed in her head, but she ignored it. She must be wrong.

"Gabrielle." He smiled slightly. "Everything has changed. I intend to make you my wife."

CHAPTER 8

*G*abrielle felt her mouth open wide, but no sound emerged.

Zavian rose and poured himself another drink. He indicated the gin. "Would you like another glass?"

"No!" She found her voice. "No," she repeated.

"Then what would you like?" He leaned back against the sideboard with a rare grin as he took a sip of his glass.

"What would I like? I'd like you to repeat what you've just said."

He drained his drink and set it on the counter.

"I'm not a diplomat, Gabrielle. I leave that to my staff. And I'm no smooth-talking womanizer. I leave that to Roshan. I'm simply a man who knows what he wants, and I want you. But I needed to clear it with the kings before I proceeded."

Gabrielle could hardly breathe. The air seemed to be sucked from the room. "I can't believe what I'm hearing!"

He frowned. "I want to make you my wife, Gabrielle. Don't you understand?"

She shook her head in disbelief and, slipping past him,

went to the French windows and gulped in the air, half expecting to see the stars had slipped, that the water had stopped flowing, that there was no perfume in the air. But it was all exactly the same.

She felt his hand on her arm. It was still sure, as if he'd done all he had to do to secure their future together. Well, he hadn't. Not by a long chalk.

"Don't you understand?" he repeated. "We will marry."

She flung off his arm and swung around. "We most certainly will not."

His brow lowered, but the certainty didn't disappear. "Why do you say that? You know we belong together. All that business of you running off with my father's money was only to make me not want you. Well, Gabrielle, you didn't succeed. Our future is together."

She swallowed down her anger. She needed to make him see. "You talk of business, of future, of success, of need. What you're talking of is a business merger."

He shrugged. "If you'd like to think of it that way—"

"I do *not* like to think of it that way!" she interrupted.

"Then what way do you like to think of it?" he asked smoothly, as if none of her anger or emotion had penetrated him. It made her even madder.

"I don't like to think of it in any way whatsoever!"

He reached out and took hold of her hand gently. She could have pulled it away if she'd wanted to, but it seemed her mental struggle didn't extend to her hand, which remained enveloped in his. He looked up and checked her stunned expression and then drew her to him with a slight tug. She bumped against him.

"You can't deny what we have," he said in a low voice that sent dangerous thrummings through her body.

She shook her head and met his gaze steadily now. "I

don't deny it. But I know it's not enough. You're no ordinary man, Zavian."

"And you're no ordinary woman."

She tugged her hand, but he refused to release it. "But don't you see?" she asked. "I am. Just that." This time he allowed her hand to go. "I'm an ordinary woman with ordinary needs and hopes."

He frowned. For the first time, the certainty was gone from his eyes. "And what are your ordinary desires?"

"To marry a man who won't come to hate me as my foreignness causes rifts in his country, or worse, war."

"That won't happen."

"I don't know on what you base this assertion because we have history, and wars all around us caused by less, which proves you're wrong."

"I will make it work."

"You alone cannot make it work." She held up her other hand to stop him from speaking, and he kissed her palm, almost making her forget what she had to say. But it was too important. "This is not about you, not about me, or an 'us', it's about your country and your people. That, Zavian, is what's important here."

"I don't deny its importance, but—"

She shook her head. "There are no buts. All you have to do is look at your parents. They married for love."

"Love?"

"Yes, love. Your father told me."

Zavian shook his head, but before he could contradict her, she continued.

"And, at first, all was well, because they didn't think your mother's English heritage would matter. But with each passing day, month, year, the pressure it created forced them apart, and forced your country apart, too. If it hadn't been for her untimely death, goodness knows what would have happened."

"That was them, this is us. Times have changed."

"Times may have changed, but your people haven't. The desert Bedouin lead the same life they've led for centuries. They still want the security of being led by a royal family of their culture and to whom they belong. Family and tribe is everything. I'm not of your family or your tribe. I'm an outsider, and I always will be."

"You're wrong. Do you think you know my people better than me? Then I will show you."

"And how exactly do you propose to do that?"

He licked his lips, and she knew he had no idea. She nodded. "You don't know because it's not possible." She sighed.

He gripped her hand as if it were a lifeline. "I *will* show you, Gabrielle. Tomorrow I will begin to show you that your life is here, with me."

She shook her head. "No. It's not just that."

His eyes narrowed. "Then what else?"

"I want to marry a man who loves me—not someone who needs me. Needs can be satisfied. Needs pass."

There was a moment when she could see the conflict in his eyes as he wrestled with things he'd never before fought with. She wondered if he would open up, if he'd acknowledge the feelings he kept a firm lid on. Because, until he did, they had no future, with or without the support of his countrymen.

But the moment passed, and the strength and purpose returned to his eyes, and she knew she'd lost him.

She tugged her hand from his, and this time he let her hand slide away. She wondered if this was a foreshadowing of what it would be like if she did what he'd said and they married. At some point he'd let her slide away, because either he didn't have any deep feelings for her, or because they were buried so deep that he didn't even know they were there, didn't even feel them anymore. She didn't know which it was, and she had no intention of staying around to find out.

She stepped outside onto the terrace without a backward glance.

ZAVIAN WATCHED her leave his room. She slipped between two gauzy curtains which trailed over her shoulder, her body dissolving into them as if into a mist, before disappearing into the darkness as if she were a part of it. As if she were a figment of his imagination.

He didn't understand her. *What had gone wrong?* He frowned as he poured himself another drink. He took one swig, scowled and threw the rest away. He didn't need a drink. There was only one thing—only one person—he needed, and that was her. The trouble was, he couldn't figure out how to get her.

He placed the glass on the table and went outside and sat where he had a view of her window, the light now turned off. He let the water and the night air soothe his spirits and mind and let his thoughts drift over his problems, teasing them, hoping they'd unravel. He closed his eyes as he imagined what Gabrielle was doing behind the dark of her closed curtains. His thoughts and feelings only tightened into a knot that would take more than the night air to undo.

He jumped up and walked inside, pausing only briefly to stare into the darkness, forcing his mind to release the mental image of Gabrielle, naked on the bed.

He might not know how to get her now, but it would come to him. It had to.

. . .

WHEN GABRIELLE HAD RECEIVED the request to attend a large formal dinner with Sheikh Mohammed—leader of a prominent and powerful Bedouin tribe—she felt conflicting feelings of both excitement and dismay. At least it wasn't going to be an intimate few. Zavian would hardly be announcing their betrothal to so many people. She accepted the invitation, only after ensuring she'd be seated at a distance from Zavian. There would be safety in numbers and safety in distance. At least she hoped so.

After dressing carefully, she walked to the reception room, from which she could hear the murmur of polite conversation and music. She smiled grimly to herself. She might have no choice but to respond to Zavian's summons, but she'd do it her way.

As Gabrielle took her seat at dinner that night, she smoothed the cloth of her new dress, regretting its glamor. When she'd placed the order for an evening dress—something she hadn't brought with her—she hadn't imagined it would be quite so sexy. At least she fitted in, she thought, looking around at the women who competed with each other to outshine with the best of New York and Paris fashions.

"He is so handsome, is he not?" a woman said to her.

Gabrielle followed the woman's gaze to the man whose lips had touched hers only days before. "Not handsome, I think."

The woman turned her shocked face to her. "Not handsome?" They both looked at the king, and the woman made a dismissive snort. "Maybe not in English terms, but he has the strength and charisma us Havilahi women admire."

Gabrielle couldn't disagree with her. 'Handsome' had never been a word she'd applied to Zavian. It was too mild. And she didn't mean it as a derogatory term as the woman had assumed.

"It is said," whispered the woman, confidentially, "that he had a love once."

Gabrielle's heart missed a beat, and she focused on taking a sip of her sparkling water. "Really? Then why isn't he marrying her?"

The woman shrugged. "No one knows. But everyone is guessing." The woman sat back with a grin. "Some say he simply grew bored." The woman looked at him with an intrigued, direct gaze as if she could devour him. "Just look at him. He could have anyone he liked." She shrugged and set her glass on the table. "Why would he settle for one?"

"Because he needs to be married, maybe?" said Gabrielle, more rattled than she should be by the woman's comments.

"But that doesn't confine him to one woman," said the woman patiently. "In our traditional culture, he can take many wives."

Gabrielle's stomach twisted with jealousy. She gritted her teeth. She never felt jealous. "I doubt he's that traditional, and I doubt that polygamy would go down well in the wider world."

"Maybe, maybe not. But I do know that at the moment there's no woman. He was to become engaged to the Tawazun sheikha, but the gossip is that that's been called off now. I've no idea why."

Gossip traveled fast. Gabrielle followed the woman's gaze to Zavian, who was deep in conversation with Sheikh Mohammed.

"He needs to marry to strengthen the country's unity, both within and without," continued the woman.

"Yes," Gabrielle said. It was exactly what she also thought. "But he needs to marry the right woman. Maybe the Tawazun sheikha wasn't the right woman."

"She was *exactly* the right woman." The woman shook her head and then turned to Gabrielle with a sneaky smile. "In one way. However, I have to say that I'm not devastated. It leaves the way open for others." She rose and smoothed down her gown. "If you get my drift." The woman winked and brazenly walked over to the table close to the king's table, bending over, obviously trying to attract his attention.

Gabrielle refused to watch. Let the king be seduced by any of the numerous women who wanted him. She didn't. Even as the thought angrily slipped into her mind, she corrected herself. No, she might want him, but she wouldn't let herself have him, not on his terms.

Someone spoke on the other side of her—an American archivist who'd been trying to attract her attention all evening—and she turned to him, glad to be distracted from the sight of women throwing themselves at Zavian.

ZAVIAN WATCHED as Gabrielle lowered her head as if intently interested in something the young American was telling her. He ground his teeth. Her hair swept the man's arm as she bowed her head to listen to him above the noise of the room. She didn't notice it, but he could tell the man did. He responded with a more intimate body language that incensed Zavian. Then it got worse. She laughed at something he said and sat back, and he could read the man's mind, seeing the woman that he saw.

It ground into his soul. Who on earth had decided to put the two of them together? He'd noticed her immediately and was annoyed that she'd managed to persuade his staff to change the seating plan. It was too late to have her moved. But at least he could observe her easily. At first, she'd looked uncomfortable, and no wonder. The other women were wearing their flashiest jewelry and clothes. And of course, Gabrielle could not compete. Even if she hadn't spent a million dollars on an artifact rather than clothes, jewelry and the like, she would never have chosen the kind of showy clothes which the women of his country preferred. She preferred to go unnoticed.

He'd watched her enter the room, her sleek form a perfect foil for the overt grandeur of the room, with its ornate golden decorations. At first, she'd been hesitant, then reserved as she'd been seated. But then she'd be in conversation with some woman who had annoyingly moved away, closer to him, allowing the man to dominate Gabrielle. It seemed the young man's smooth flirtations had amused her, and she positively glowed. He growled.

"What is it, Your Majesty?" his vizier asked under his breath.

Zavian glanced at his too perceptive advisor. "That young American. Have him called away."

The vizier's expression darkened. "And Dr. Taylor brought here, no doubt. I warn you that—"

Zavian waved his hand. "No more warnings, Naseer. I've had enough to last me a miserable lifetime."

"It might be miserable, but at least it will be a peaceful and prosperous one."

Zavian didn't need to speak any further. The vizier beckoned an assistant who had soon called the baffled looking American away from dinner on an errand.

Zavian returned his attention to his honored guest, who was seated to his right. He didn't need to see his instructions carried out; he could visualize Gabrielle's reaction. The laughter would have gone, and her expression would be guarded once more. But what did that matter? He didn't wish to inspire laughter, the opposite in fact. He wished her to be serious and to understand her future was here, with him.

ZAVIAN TALKED EASILY with his honored guest as if he weren't aware of the moment when Gabrielle slipped into the newly vacated seat beside him—arranged subtly by his vizier—and sat ramrod straight as if she'd been inserted into the scene without wishing to be a part of it.

He glanced around the room and noted how people—especially the woman who had been seated beside Gabrielle before—were all now staring at her. He turned his attention back to his honored guest. Gabrielle would have to get used to that. Being stared at went with the job.

It was only when Zavian introduced the sheikh to someone that he could withdraw from the conversation and turn to his other side. She sat still, a tight polite half-smile on her face like a mask. It didn't fool him.

"Dr. Taylor." Zavian nodded.

"Your Majesty," she answered formally, flicking him a quick wary look.

"How good of you to join me."

"Good?" Her smile squeezed tighter around her lips. "You commanded me to come. Apparently, none of my excuses were acceptable."

He bit back the flare of irritation. He wouldn't rise to the bait. "And why would you wish to make an excuse?" He nodded to a passing acquaintance and settled his gaze on her.

"Because there are just the two of us. I have no wish to sit beside the king, to create gossip over nothing."

"Nothing? I think not." He didn't wait for her to reply. "Would you care for a drink? Wine, whiskey, liqueur?"

"A cup of tea, please."

"Tea," he repeated, unable to prevent his disapproving tone. It was obvious she was more interested in emphasizing the differences between them than identifying the similarities. A waiter responded to his raised brows, and he ordered the tea.

"Yes, tea," she said, her smile relaxing as she felt she'd won a point. "I am English, after all."

He tried not to rise to the bait but failed. "I like whiskey, but I'm not Scottish or Irish."

Her eyes narrowed. One all. He took a deep breath. He could be gracious in victory. "I hope you've enjoyed your evening?"

"Of course." She smiled politely. "I've been in very pleasant company... up until now."

His smile faded instantly as he followed her gaze to the young American archivist who'd returned and reciprocated her smile.

"Would you like your new 'friend' to join us?" He gave her a look so that she'd know exactly what her friend would get if he dared to accept an invitation to the king's table.

She shook her head quickly, and his gaze lowered to her bit lip. Such beautiful lips—plump and red. They were not meant to be bitten, but to be kissed. Her slender shoulders rose and fell, shifting the sheen of the satin dress, which shimmered in the light, highlighting her curves. "No, thank you. I'm sure he's fine where he is."

"Really," pressed Zavian, unable to stop himself now. "He's most welcome to join us. I'd be interested in asking him—"

"Interrogating him," Gabrielle interrupted.

Zavian ignored her. "Asking him all about his work." He sat back. "You know how interested I am in his work."

"What work is that?" asked the Bedouin sheikh, who'd just turned around after finishing his conversation.

Zavian stifled his irritation at being interrupted in a conversation with Gabrielle, which, despite its prickliness, he found compelling. "The celebration of poetry."

Gabrielle looked at him sharply. Zavian smiled at her.

"You thought I didn't know about a celebration of poetry in the desert?"

She shrugged. "I didn't…" She trailed off.

Zavian turned with a smile once more to the honored Bedouin guest. "May I introduce Dr. Gabrielle Taylor, Sheikh Mohammed?"

Sheikh Mohammed smiled. "Gabrielle and I are friends of old, are we not, Gabrielle?"

Zavian tried to keep his smile in place. He hadn't known that Sheikh Mohammed knew Gabrielle. It seemed there was no end to the surprises for him this evening.

"Indeed," Gabrielle said, with the first genuine smile of the evening. "My earliest memory of you was when my grandfather was working in your village."

Mohammed nodded and smiled. "He changed everything for us. Put us on the map. I owe your grandfather a debt of gratitude I can never repay."

"He didn't see it that way." Gabrielle shrugged. "Besides, he's gone now."

Mohammed leaned in toward Gabrielle, ignoring Zavian. "And the world lost a great man with his passing, but…" He sat back again, considering Gabrielle and then Zavian thoughtfully. "But, the debt remains. But it is to you now, rather than your grandfather."

Gabrielle smiled. "You owe me nothing, sir."

"On the contrary. If there's ever anything I can do for you, all you have to do is contact me, and I will do my best to help."

"That is very kind of you, sir, but I assure you there is no debt either to my grandfather or myself."

He grimaced slightly. "You surely wouldn't prevent an old man from repaying his debt?"

"No, of course not."

"Good."

Zavian cleared his throat. "And your family are all well, Mohammed?"

Mohammed rested his eagle glance on Zavian.

"They are, Your Majesty. My wife thrives with her children and grandchildren all around her. Our life follows the traditional pattern and continues as my father and his father before him."

"Tradition is everything," Gabrielle said.

Mohammed smiled, but Zavian didn't. Gabrielle was scoring another point. The comment was aimed at him, not Mohammed, who had turned away to respond to a waiter's query.

"Tradition is not everything, Gabrielle," said Zavian in a low voice, hoping Mohammed wouldn't hear. But then Mohammed turned to them both.

Mohammed turned first one bushy-browed perceptive glance to Gabrielle before his gaze rested on Zavian. "Tradition is a complex thing, Zavian," he said, dropping the formal title he'd been using all evening. "It can be changed and renewed, but it must always have an essence, don't you think?" The old man turned to Gabrielle. "An essence, Gabrielle, is required. But the question is, what comprises that essence?" He smiled and stood up.

"You're leaving so soon?" asked Gabrielle, her heartfelt, genuine regret obvious. Zavian just wished she sounded so heartfelt with him. If Mohammed hadn't been old enough to be her grandfather, he would have been jealous.

"I am, my dear. We will be returning to my homeland early. But I hope you will be able to join us at our celebration of poetry." What was the old man doing? Zavian saw the brief look of confusion on Gabrielle's face. She recovered quickly.

"It would be my honor as well as my pleasure."

"Good, then I will expect you as part of the royal entourage. That is all right, isn't it, Zavian?"

Zavian hadn't thought to invite Gabrielle to such an event. It was small, insignificant and he was only attending because of his ties to Mohammed and his family. "Of course."

"Good," replied Mohammed, looking back at Gabrielle once more. "And I hope that maybe I can repay that debt of mine."

Gabrielle smiled, but a frown settled as she watched the old man walk away.

But Zavian didn't frown. He felt his spirits lighten. As he watched Mohammed, Zavian thought for the first time that the old man might be on his side. He was going to look forward to this poetry celebration.

CHAPTER 9

*G*abrielle looked around the group of people ranged around the campfire and wondered how she could have borne to be away for so long.

As the sun began to slide behind the inky horizon, with the humps and rolls of the sand dunes all around the camp, encircling and cosseting them like a nurturing mother, the chanting of the *Al-Taghrooda* began.

First, the haunting strains of the *rababa* filled the air, the bow drawn back and forth over the strings, while the player's fingers move quickly over holes in the pipe at the top. Then a man's voice rose and fell as he honored his home and family with his poetry. No sooner had his voice faded, than another answered him, responding to his words, affirming their traditions—shared history and friends and companions, traveling across the deserts in a camel train. They were words that had been passed down through the generations by the community of elders.

The poets may have arrived by car, and the few camels grazed some distance away, but the sentiments were as relevant today as they had been over the centuries that the oral tradition had continued.

A lump came into Gabrielle's throat, which she tried unsuccessfully to swallow, as tears sprung to her eyes. She blinked furiously. She wanted no one to see, particularly Zavian. Seated with the women, who'd be performing their own *Al-Taghrooda* later, she glanced at where he sat with the other men.

Zavian listened attentively, but she immediately noticed he had a different expression on his face than usual. His jaw was less tense, his eyes less guarded. She snatched in a short breath and returned her gaze to the poets, scarcely taking in the short movements of the poet's whip—a reference to their heritage as camel riders—which marked patterns in the sand, emphasizing their poetry.

Somehow she'd managed to avoid seeing Zavian alone over the few days since the dinner with Sheikh Mohammed. Other than her work, she'd kept to her room, and even Zavian had drawn the line at seeking her out there. Which was good because she had nothing to say to him. She was back to square one. Zavian wanting her but not loving her, and she, a misfit in the country she loved so much.

But today she'd pushed aside any thought of being a misfit, to enjoy the traditional poetry which made her feel at one with this country.

Then silence fell, and it was time for Gabrielle and the women to perform. She'd felt honored to be asked, as it was a privilege to participate. After a couple of women had recited their poetry, it was her turn. Although acutely aware of her difference to the women—taller and paler, as well as her accent—by the time it was her turn, she was lost in the words she recited, all thought of nerves vanished.

She didn't rise but, like the others, sat around the circle. The women's poetry—Nabati poetry—focused more on the domestic world than the men's. And the poem she'd chosen by a poetess called Bakhu Al-Mariyah was no different. It expressed, in Arabic, the poet's longing for a tent and an over-riding love for the desert which called to Gabrielle above everything. It described how her gaze would rest on the "plain behind the mountain" where the Bedouin nomads would be making their desert camps.

There were nods of approval for the poem's sentiments and for her delivery, and then another poet began to perform. As she sat back and listened, the last words she'd spoken echoed in her mind, and she couldn't help wondering if Zavian had received the message which lay behind her choice of the poem. Her heart belonged to freedom and the desert, not tied down to one place, one man, especially with a man who had no love for her.

The *dallah* was taken from the burning embers of the fire, which were re-ignited, bursting a welcome warmth around the space. A woman poured hot water from the *dallah* into a tray of glasses, and the aroma from the sage-flavored tea rose into the air.

Gabrielle took a sip of the sweet tea, washing away the taste of the roast goat. The colors of the flags which draped the outside of the tent, together with the traditional patterns of the inside, muted as the sun disappeared and a swift twilight followed, lit only by the fire and lanterns.

Sheikh Mohammed spoke to Zavian, and he beckoned her over with a smile. With the formal part of the evening now over, people were moving around, greeting old friends. Gabrielle rose and greeted the sheikh.

"Gabrielle!" Mohammed said with a smile, cutting through her formal greeting. "Come, sit by my side."

As Gabrielle sat between Zavian and the chief, more refreshments were brought, and she studiously looked at the tea rather than meet Zavian's gaze which seared her cheeks.

"Thank you, Gabrielle, for your poem," Mohammed continued.

"You're most welcome."

"I, for one, appreciate your patriotism. For someone not of our country, you certainly share a deep love and appreciation for it. You show a loyalty to our land and people which some of our own people would do well to emulate."

"I'm deeply honored you should think so, and also to be invited."

"You need no invitation from me to return to your spiritual home, Gabrielle," Mohammed said.

As her host's attention was caught by one of his grandchildren, Gabrielle took a sip of her tea and pondered the old man's words. She felt it to be her home. And Zavian had said as much.

The flames of the firelight flickered into focus the paintings on the stone walls, which rose around them. The geometric designs of the tents under the towering palm trees shifted slightly in the night breeze. The smell of the blooms, large and white, hung heavily in the air.

"Your 'spiritual home,'" Mohammed said. 'A patriot,' 'loyal to our land and people'." Gabrielle turned to Zavian. He wasn't looking at her, but gazing across the scene, at the people drinking, eating and talking. His face was rimmed with gold by the firelight.

"He's an old friend of my grandfather's."

He turned to her sharply, and she could see a spark of anger and frustration in his eyes. "And what does that mean? That he says such things out of affection alone?" He leaned toward her, and his eyes darkened, transforming the anger into something quite different. "No, Gabrielle, he says them because they are true."

She gritted her teeth, steeling herself against the onslaught. "Just look at me, Zavian."

"I am." And he was, more than she was comfortable with, but she'd invited it.

"And what do you see?" She didn't wait for him to answer. "A woman who looks and sounds very different from anyone else here." She shook her head.

"Really, Gabrielle? You would not say such things of other people! You would not judge people in such a superficial, unimportant way as you have just described!"

She sucked in air to respond, but his words stopped her. Instead, she tore her gaze from him as the truth of his words repeated in her brain, bombarding her defenses. The darting flames of the fire distorted the people's faces on the far side of the space, and she turned quickly away from them, looking across to where one of the women she'd been seated with earlier gave her a warm smile which bloomed across her face, encompassing Gabrielle within it. She swallowed and smiled back before looking up at the dark, inky sky, but it held no relief from her thoughts. The stars stared right down at her as if accusing her with the same direct views as Zavian.

She felt his hand on her arm. "Gabrielle," he said softly, but she refused to turn to his word or touch.

She shook her head. "Don't. It's impossible."

His hand squeezed around her arm, gripping it with an intensity that did make her turn to him. "You are a stubborn woman. What do I have to do, what do any of us have to do, to make you see clearly?"

"Don't you understand, Zavian? I daren't see clearly. It's my last defense."

"Defense from what?"

She shrugged. "From rejection, I guess." She looked down at his hand, which still gripped her arm. It suddenly occurred to her that she didn't know if he was gripping her arm like a lifeline, to be saved, or whether it was for her own benefit.

"Do I look like I'm rejecting you? Do I sound as if I'm rejecting you? Does anything I've done appear like that?"

"I know you want me now." She didn't tell him that she also knew why he wanted her. He wanted her because they couldn't be near each other without wanting each other. But that was physical and ephemeral. "But it's not enough to build a future on."

"I say it is." His undertone revealed a savage desperation that surprised her. "I need you, Gabrielle. You connect me to my country like no one else can."

Something nagged at her mind. "When were you last here?"

He pressed his lips together. "Since I was last with you."

"With *me?*" she repeated incredulously. "Are you seriously telling me you haven't been back to be with these people for over a year?"

He nodded and looked away. "I could not bear it."

This got to her like nothing else had been able to do. "Zavian." She placed her hand over his, which still lay on hers. He turned his around and captured hers, dropping it out of sight, beneath the table. His fingers explored hers, stroking along the length of hers, his eyes studying its progress as if mesmerized.

He looked up, and she could have sworn there were tears in his eyes if she hadn't known better. The King of Gharb Havilah didn't ever cry, and nor did her ex-lover, Zavian.

"Your hands are working hands," he said with a strange gentleness.

She laughed, the tension broken by his words. "I see your gift for giving compliments hasn't changed." The laughter settled into a smile on her lips. It had no reflection in his own serious expression.

"I've never been good with words, you know that. It's always been you who has possessed that gift." He brought her hand up to the firelight, apparently uncaring if anyone should see. "But I *do* mean it as a compliment." He slid his fingers up and down hers. "I remember watching you dig in the sands of the desert, and then at night..." Their gazes tangled for a moment as she wondered what he was going to describe. "Then, at night, your hardened fingers would hit the keys of your grandfather's ancient typewriter, as you finished your work."

"No electricity in the desert," she replied softly.

He pulled her hand away and held it within both of his, carefully, examining it like a treasure which it was. He brought it up to the light. "I missed your hand."

"Just my hand?"

She'd dipped her head to see his face better. He shook his head. "No, not just your hand." He raised her hand to his lips and kissed it, keeping her hand close, as he inhaled her as if she were a perfume.

She laughed uncertainly. "Don't tell me you missed the way I speak to you? Like a human being, rather than an acolyte?"

He raised an eyebrow. "No, I don't miss that. Why would I miss someone who fails to give Gharb Havilah royalty the respect it deserves?"

"Ah, now there you've got it wrong. I respect Gharb Havilah royalty greatly. I just don't respect stupidity."

He huffed a half-laugh at her direct response. "Are you calling me stupid, Dr. Taylor?"

Her grin faded on her lips. "Not stupid. Never stupid, maybe misguided." She searched his face, still with that strange, gentle expression she hadn't seen before. "Lost, even," she added.

The gentleness was immediately replaced by a frowning indignance. "You think I'm lost? Whatever gives you that idea? It is I who am king of this country where I have lived my whole life, among my family, among my people. Why on earth would you think I was lost?"

"Because you cling to rules and regulations and principles for dear life. If they slip from your grasp, where will you be? Adrift? Floundering? Out of control?"

He ground his teeth. "You are letting your imagination run away with you. My life is ordered because it is most efficient that way. I don't expect you to understand this. Your life has always been lived in chaos."

A look of regret passed over his face, and he opened his mouth to speak but shook his head instead. She slipped her hand out of his, and he didn't try to stop her. He turned and called for a refill of his coffee.

"I thought you missed my honest speech," she said quietly.

He glanced at her before holding up his cup to be refilled. "Only up to a point."

"And that point being no further than you can accept. Not beyond your own understanding."

"Enough!" he said. People looked around at his raised voice. His eyes closed briefly before nodding reassurance to those around him. "I'm not here to argue."

"Tell me, Zavian, truthfully, why do you want me?"

"Is it not enough that I *do* want you?"

"No."

He frowned. "Not enough that a day hasn't gone by since you left, without me dreaming of you, or imagining you, your kiss, your touch, you in my arms, in my bed?"

She swallowed and shook her head.

"Gabrielle! You cannot deny what we have."

She couldn't deal with this anymore. "I don't," she said, jumping up and looking around. The desert had always been her escape, her world where she felt safe, but now she felt exposed and confused. "I have to go."

He rose, ignoring the curious looks from others. The

music drowned out their words. "Not like this, please. I didn't intend to drive you away. Quite the opposite. Please, sit down, and let's talk." His grip on her hand tightened. "Please, I need to be clear about why I brought you here from Oxford."

She nodded reluctantly, intrigued despite herself, and sat down. "Okay, tell me what you need to tell me, and then I'm going to bed."

He nodded and drew in a deep breath. Gabrielle could feel the effort it was taking him to do this.

"You know I arranged it all."

She nodded. "Yes, I know now. At first, I didn't."

"And that was because I didn't mean you to. But what you don't know is why."

"I have a good idea."

He held up his hand. "Let me tell you. I'd arranged it to get you out of my system." She blanched, recoiled, but he didn't stop. "I hated the fact I wanted you so much. That you wouldn't leave my mind. And, I thought, it was because of lack. A question of simple economics—supply and demand." She shook her head in disbelief. "If the supply was there—"

"Me, being the supply?" she asked, incredulous.

He nodded. "Then the demand—"

"Your need for me."

"Would diminish, yes. But it didn't work. I'd forgotten to factor into my plan certain things."

"What things?" She could hear the sharp edge of anger in her voice but did nothing to stop it.

He dipped his head closer to her cheek and breathed in. "Things like your fragrance. Apparently, the law of economics doesn't apply to fragrance."

She softened slightly and couldn't prevent a smile from tugging at the corners of her mouth. She was about to reply, but his thumb swept across her cheekbone as his gaze deepened into her eyes.

"Nor the luminous look in your eyes." His eyes pinched at the corners as if trying to understand something inexplicable. "It's... unquantifiable."

The last of her tension left her and Gabrielle laughed. She shook her head. "I'm a woman, Zavian," she said gently. "I'm not a thing, a box to be ticked or crossed off. People are far more complex than that."

His frown deepened for a second and then lightened, and he did something she didn't expect. He smiled. "Apparently. Particularly you."

"Particularly when there are feelings involved."

He rose and offered her his hand, and slowly she stood up. The palm fronds clattered overhead, and the night breeze quickened, bringing with it the scent of blossom. There were few people left seated around the fire now, but those that were glanced briefly up at them and smiled before returning to their reveries and conversation.

"You want me to come to your bed?" she asked.

"Only if you also want it."

"I want to, make no mistake about that. It's whether I *should* is the question."

"What can I say to help you make up your mind?"

"Nothing."

"Then I will *do* something to forget your thoughts." With that, he slid his fingers through her hair and brought her head to his and kissed her. From the moment his lips touched hers, and she felt the sharp intake of his breath the hard knot of tangled thoughts unraveled. It was a kiss which obliterated all thought—both his and hers. It seemed, while people might be more complex, there were some things about them which were simple.

He pulled her close, as he explored her mouth with his

tongue, his lips with hers, and caressed her cheek as he held her steady as if scared she'd run away. It was the last thing on her mind. It was as if he'd struck a match and tossed it into a landscape starved of water—a desert of emotion—and one which exploded at the first sign of fire. And there was nowhere else either of them could go now, except to feed that fire.

He gripped her hand, and they dissolved into the shadows away from the flickering firelight, unnoticed by the few who remained sleeping or drinking before the fire.

They wove their way through the tents until they reached his and entered the shadowy interior, lit by oil lamps, which shed a rich light onto the rugs and decorations which lined the tent.

Their hands were upon each other immediately, tugging at their clothes, slipping beneath the layers to feel the warmth and contours of each other's bodies. Within moments they were stripped of their robes and underclothes, and Zavian carried her naked to the bed, lit only by a side-light of brass lamps.

She took his hand and pulled him down to her, and they kissed as she wrapped her legs around him. With one swift movement, he was inside her. She cried out, and her head fell back as he pushed further, filling her completely.

He held her face, his eyes searching hers as if needing to know something only her body could tell him, as he thrust rhythmically into her. What he wanted to know from her, she couldn't tell, but as she watched his expression change and intensify, she knew that, whatever he didn't say, he was hers.

The thought gave her power, and she writhed in his arms, determined to break down the barrier he refused to drop and make him see what was before his eyes. Her. Not a woman to own, or to dominate, but a woman to love.

But in the end, it was her own barriers which dissolved under his skillful lovemaking, and she came first, her whole body—from the tips of her toes to her fingers—tingling as the orgasm rolled and coiled inside her and then doubled again as he came, filling her with himself.

They lay gaining their breath for a few moments, and then she slid on top of him, determined to gain the upper hand. After a long lingering kiss, he was ready for her again, and she sat astride him and slipped slowly onto him.

ZAVIAN WATCHED as Gabrielle rose and fell, her breasts peaked and rosy under the warm lamplight, her hair in messy disarray around her shoulders, and her eyelids fluttering closed. Her movement were so sensuous, so natural, so instinctive, so primeval that the setting seemed perfect. The flickering candles encased in their brass lanterns cast her moving shadows across the undulating walls of the tent, which moved slightly with the quickening breeze.

The music continued outside, the strains of the stringed violin echoing their own passion. Gabrielle rose and fell with the vibration of the music floating in on the wind. It felt as if they were one. Zavian was no longer aware of anything except for Gabrielle, at the center of the maelstrom of passion, her tight, wet body encasing him, shifting against him, his hands caressing her skin, his eyes drinking in the beauty of her slender body, so slight and yet so powerful. His control was fracturing at the onslaught of her power. He saw the moment she orgasmed, her body and face lit up with an ecstasy that was ethereal, other-worldly. And he desperately wanted to bring her back into his world.

She leaned over, her breasts brushing against his chest, and kissed him. He put his arms around her and their kiss deepened. As one they rolled over, and he withdrew and took satisfaction at the corresponding jerky movements of her body, as she reacted to his thrusts. He threaded his fingers through hers and spread her arms wide, pinioning with his hips, taking his pleasure just as she'd taken hers. Except this was no one-sided pleasure. It was as if they were one entity, each movement, each thought, each feeling echoed in the other, felt by the other.

Slowly, imperceptibly, they inched their way to the brink. Their eyes fastened onto each other with an urgency and intensity as if holding onto each other in a turbulent sea to save each other. They came as one, his seed spilling deep inside her, claiming her for his own. She opened her mouth in a soft moan, and his lips found hers.

He rolled to his side, Gabrielle captured tight in his arms, and he kissed her hair, her forehead, her closed eyelids. Then he settled back. There were no words between them because they'd communicated far more than words could. But as the music stopped and the wind picked up, and sand crept under the tent, reality seeped back in, and a sullen dread filtered through Zavian's consciousness. His arms didn't loosen their hold of Gabrielle, but his mind shifted away.

What had he done? He'd thought to bring her to Gharb Havilah, he'd thought to seduce her, to rid himself of the memories of her which had haunted his every waking and sleeping moment since she'd left him. He'd thought to cauterize the pain she'd caused by proving to himself that it was ephemeral, that it was a residue, a ghost in his mind which would be extinguished. Except it hadn't.

Like some wandering seed, it had, instead, lodged deep inside of him, and it had proved not to be uprooted so easily. Indeed, it had blossomed. He could feel the tentacles of her growing inside, trying to take over his body and mind. The thought of being taken over, being under the control of someone else, terrified him.

He swallowed as he moved first his hand, then his arm from her body. She was fast asleep, but she shivered and snuggled against him. He closed his eyes and grimaced as he freed himself again. This time she didn't move. Her breathing was regular, and a soft, rosy blush lay on her cheeks.

He shook his head and slowly got dressed. He wanted her in his life, of that he was clear now. The trouble was, she wanted something he couldn't give. Because how could you give your heart when it was made of stone? His own hard heart lay between him and happiness, and there was nothing he could do about it.

CHAPTER 10

*G*abrielle wasn't sure where she was when her eyes flickered open to a gray and shadowy pre-dawn light that barely penetrated the tent. She'd dreamt she was with her grandfather after a day's digging in the desert. That the fire had died down and they were talking with ease about everything under the moon before they retired to bed. The same sense of comfort and rest and love had settled over her, calming her unquiet spirit. The same feeling was still with her as she looked around, trying to make out the shapes of things within the tent to place herself. Then she heard a rustle of clothing, and she turned to see a dark shape of a man coming towards her. She wasn't scared. She knew in an instant that it was Zavian, and everything else fell into place.

"You're awake," he said. There was a rasping sound as he struck a match and lit a candle before placing the brass cover back on the lantern. He stayed there for a few seconds, adjusting the flame, his face lit randomly by the darting flame, one moment casting his face into shadow, his strong features softened, the next highlighting the whites of his eyes, distorting his familiar features until he looked like the very devil. The thought made her sit up, now wide awake.

"Just," she replied. "What time is it?" She groped in the shadows for her phone.

"Before dawn. I wanted to speak with you before the world awoke."

She felt a flutter of nerves in her stomach. She sat up more and leaned back against the soft pillows, drawing the cover to hide her nakedness. "That sounds... serious."

He smiled an enigmatic smile that told her nothing. "And I've brought coffee."

"Um, you're trying to soften me now, before you get to the serious stuff."

"Maybe." He passed her a cup.

She breathed it in, closing her tired eyes against the steam, feeling invigorated simply from inhaling its strength. She took a sip. "Well, it's working."

He sat down—not close to her, she noticed—but made no attempt to drink his own coffee. "Good. Then perhaps we can begin."

"Begin... what?"

"To talk about our future. After last night you can no longer deny your future is here, in Gharb Havilah. You are accepted by our people, and you are accepted by me."

His plainly spoken words fell like a challenge between them both. She placed her cup onto the side table with a shaking hand and swung her legs off the bed, still clutching the covers around her.

"On second thoughts, perhaps I should be dressed before you throw important questions at me." She rose and walked over to where her clothes were scattered.

She heard a sigh from behind her. "You think your clothes will protect you from my questions?"

"No," she said, deliberately dropping the awkward cover

to pull on her top. If he thought he could side-swipe her with difficult questions, she *knew* she could divert him with one simple movement.

And, if his silence was anything to go by, it had worked. A shower would have to wait. Only when she was dressed did she turn around. And, yes, from his expression, she knew his thoughts had strayed. His eyes were dark, liquid and his lips were parted as if he imagined pressing them against her. She shivered.

He jumped up. "I'm sorry, you are cold. Please, drink your coffee." He went and got a soft throw and gently pulled it around her shoulders. "Your clothes might not have protected you, but your nakedness very nearly did." He kissed her gently and then withdrew back to his chair. "Nearly, but not quite. I repeat you're acceptable to us both— my country and me—and you must see that now."

"Acceptable," she repeated with a soft grunt. "Now, that's quite a word. Practically guaranteed to make a woman change her mind."

He frowned, the darting shadows falling heavily now around his eyes and below his cheekbones. He looked... dangerous. But it didn't matter how dangerous he looked, she wasn't about to surrender herself to a man who found her simply "acceptable".

"And what word, Gabrielle, would you prefer? Something suitably sentimental, like love?"

She shrugged, as if nonchalant, as if that word wasn't the fulcrum of her life and her future. "It certainly has the ring of tradition about it. It's usually mentioned when a man tells a woman she should stay with him."

"Not this man. You should know by now that love is irrelevant to me. It has no meaning."

She approached him. "It does if you have a heart."

"Ah," he said, his eyes still hard, despite the way she drew her head closer to his. "Now there is the crux of the problem. I have no heart. Only a body and a mind—both of which want you, no, *need* you to stay."

She shook her head. "You *have* a heart, Zavian, whether you like it or not."

He shook his head. "Only one which pumps blood around my body. It's a functional heart, not a sentimental one. And why do you insist on this point? You are a scientist and believe only what can be proved."

"And love can be proved, *and* it endures when all else fails."

He grunted in disbelief and shook his head again, shifting in his seat. She knew he hated to discuss such things. She decided to press her advantage. "Thoughts and beliefs change, lust burns out—"

"But you think love lasts forever, hey?" He drank back his coffee. There was movement now from outside the tent. People had risen and were going to pray. He stood up. "You are innocent to believe such a thing."

"You're wrong. I have seen and felt too much in my life to be innocent, too much to *not* believe in love. It's the *only* thing I have faith in. I might belong, but only to the country, not to you. I can't be with you. I cannot trust someone who doesn't love me, someone who I don't even know can love."

A tense silence fell. "I don't know if I can love, either, Gabrielle."

"Then you need to find out. Because, while I might stay here in this land—because you're right, it *is* my home, and last night showed me that people I respect and admire, believe it to be my home, also—I can't be with you, not with a man who doesn't know his own heart."

She stepped away and opened the flap to the tent where the sun rose at the same time as the call to prayer filled the air. She looked back. "You're afraid, I get that." He shook his head, incensed at the idea that he might be afraid. She held up her hand, something she never did, and his words died in his mouth with surprise. "But until you face your fears and figure out your feelings"—she tapped her heart—"what you have, here, then there is no way forward—for either of us."

She didn't wait for an answer but swiftly left the camp and secured transport for her return to the city. He might have got what he wanted from the trip into the desert, but she'd left him with something to think about.

Part of her had wanted to cave in and be with him. She loved him, and she loved this land. But she'd done enough soul searching over the past year to know that it wasn't enough. Until he allowed her into his heart, their relationship had no future. He'd got it quite wrong. It was the other thing, lust, which was ephemeral. That could end, and if and when it did, so would their relationship. It was only love which endured. Her grandfather had taught her that.

It HAD all gone spectacularly wrong. For a man who prided himself on careful calculation, he'd completely misjudged the situation. Zavian picked up a pen and tapped it on the table, irritated beyond belief that instead of ridding himself of an obsession, being with Gabrielle had only increased it, creating a panic inside of himself which he'd managed to tie into a knot since he'd returned from his night in the desert. He refused to indulge it.

The tapping increased in intensity until he slid the pen away from him and jumped up from the table and strode to the window. He was suddenly aware of a silence which had descended on the room. He turned and glared at the people seated at the board table, aware that he had no idea what they'd been talking to him about.

"The meeting is concluded."

There was avoidance of his gaze and some mutterings. His vizier frowned and picked up his papers. The others looked to him for guidance in their confusion but he gestured for them to leave. Naseer watched the door close and only then approached Zavian.

"Your Majesty," he began.

Zavian raised his eyebrow. "Formality. This must be serious."

"When you cannot concentrate in a policy meeting, it *is* serious."

Zavian grunted and continued to look straight out to the distant horizon, toward the desert where his thoughts remained. "There was nothing being discussed that needed my comment."

"Everything needs your comment."

"You do not need to lecture me on the responsibilities of kingship, Naseer."

"Unfortunately, it appears I do. You've brought that chit of a girl into our country, against my wishes I may add, and carry on with her as if you're a teenager. Allah only knows why you brought her back into your life again."

He turned to his trusted vizier and not for the first time wished he was a little less wise and bit more supportive. "Do you want to know why I brought her here? Hey?" He didn't wait for a reply. "Because I needed to rid myself of her. Absence didn't work, so I thought familiarity might."

"And did it?"

Zavian turned away again, back to the view of minarets and spires and towers mysterious in the soft, hazy light of early morning. "No." His vizier gave a heavy sigh and turned away. It seemed this conundrum had even flummoxed his wily old advisor. "No words of wisdom, eh Naseer? No advice? No wise words about troubles of the heart?"

Naseer paused and looked away. In that one single movement, Zavian knew for sure. He turned to him.

"You put her up to it, didn't you?"

If there had been any doubt in Zavian's mind, it was wiped away when Naseer looked him in the eye. There was guilt, recognition of truth, but also something else, defiance. "Yes, I suggested it to your father as the only way out. Your father was a dying man, and with your brother gone, I knew you were the future. But not with her. You needed a suitable wife." He waved his hand. "Not an English academic."

"She's more than that," Zavian said quietly.

For the first time ever, Naseer bit his lip, and his eyes shifted, betraying his lack of certainty. Eventually, he nodded. "Yes, maybe she is. But at the time, your father and I saw her departure as the best thing for your country, and you."

"And now?"

"Now"—Naseer forgot about royal etiquette and sat wearily on the chair next to Zavian—"I'm beginning to think I might have misjudged the situation, and Dr. Taylor."

"You think you did the wrong thing."

Naseer nodded but couldn't meet Zavian's eye. "Dr. Taylor is most... unusual. Sometimes I listen to what she's saying, and I can hardly believe she's not of our lineage. When I listen to my granddaughters speak of frivolous things, I could only wish that they had a quarter of Dr. Taylor's commitment to Gharb Havilah. My advice? Marry her."

"That's some turnaround." He rose and strode to the window. "But what about love?"

Naseer scoffed, just as Zavian had known he would, reflecting his own thoughts. "You talk of love?" he asked, incredulous. "This isn't about such a fancy." He dismissed the notion with a wave of his hand. "And I cannot advise you on such matters. I have no knowledge of the affairs of the heart. I only know they can derail people from their purpose. And your purpose, may I remind you, Zavian, is to head a country of ten million people, numerous conflicting tribes, and resist international inroads on our port. We are at a strategic part of the world that the superpowers wish to control. The country is at the center of global power, and you are at the country's center. It all depends on you. Love is not a factor in any of these things."

"I am aware."

"And you must also be aware that marriage is crucial, and your Dr. Taylor appears to be the only woman of whom Sheikh Mohammed approves. And if Mohammed approves, then you'll have the support of others. "

Naseer put a hand on Zavian's shoulder, and Zavian turned to him, surprised. His vizier rarely touched him. He was a supremely intelligent man, a master chess player, and a man he'd never seen cry or express any form of emotion. A man who'd only made physical contact with Zavian a few times over their long relationship. Once when he'd been a child and had got into a fight with street kids. Zavian had lost his temper, and it had only been his vizier's touch which had dissipated the mist and allowed him to see clearly again. And then when his mother had died, and grief had threatened to overwhelm him. Both times, Zavian realized, were when Zavian's emotions had threatened to gain a hold over him. And now this.

"She doesn't wish to marry me."

It appeared he'd found a way to floor Naseer. He poked his old head forward, his brows knitted in bewilderment. "What?"

"Gabrielle does not wish to marry me."

"Then she is a fool."

"We both know she isn't that."

The vizier's frown hadn't lessened, but he nodded. "She has a weakness. A sentimentality that has no part in ruling a country. But..." His vizier paused as the frown lifted and his eyes brightened. "But," he repeated with a shrug, "such sentimentality is a small thing. This weakness, Zavian"—he waved his hand in dismissal—"can be addressed. Do whatever you have to do to make her marry you. Promise whatever you have to."

"I can become someone I am not."

"You have no choice. Time is running out. An announcement of some sort has been made at the bi-millenial celebrations and an announcement there will be."

Naseer left the room without waiting for a response from Zavian, which was just as well because Zavian was confounded. He'd assumed his vizier would come up with a way out of their predicament. But it seemed there was no going back. He wanted Gabrielle, and his country and advisors wished him to marry Gabrielle. The only stumbling block was Gabrielle. She wanted love, and he couldn't deliver love.

He slammed the laptop closed with a snap and walked out the room. His vizier had been wrong once before, and he was wrong again. Naseer underestimated Gabrielle, something Zavian did not. She wouldn't change her mind. She was as stubborn as her grandfather. Once her heart and mind were made up, they were as one and couldn't be changed.

If he had to do without her, then so would his country. Both would survive. It's just that he'd hoped for something more than survival.

GABRIELLE SQUINTED as she moved the object to the bright mid-day light streaming in the museum window. Yes, it was definitely from the same period as the other. She replaced it gently into its case and made a few notes on her laptop. She rubbed a remaining trace of sand from the object between her fingertips, and her mind was instantly back in the desert, with Zavian.

She wished it wasn't. Whenever she thought of him she felt hurt, literally, from the tingle in her fingertips to the sinking in her gut. Her love for him created a visceral, physical response in her. Pity it was one-sided. Zavian had made it clear that he didn't and couldn't love her. She didn't believe him. She *knew* him. *She. Knew. Him.* Like he didn't know himself. He'd been forced to draw shutters around his heart from an early age, to keep it caged, imprisoned, somewhere deep inside where it couldn't hurt him. His parents had done that to him, and even the love he'd received from his grandfather had been a chill affair, trained into external accomplishments, hunting, physical things which further worked to hide his emotions so well that now he didn't know they existed. He gave them different names, different attributes. He was lying to himself, and only he could discover the truth.

She sat away from the screen and rubbed her tired eyes. Only one more week to go before she could leave and return to her Oxford position, her college no longer in financial trouble. And her? She had a feeling her trouble was only just beginning. But it was something she'd have to learn how to live with.

The phone buzzed, and she answered it. "Okay," she said with a sigh. She tried to muster a smile. It wasn't the TV crew's fault she hated publicity. "No problem. I'll be right there."

She rose and swept her hands down her clothes and checked her face in the mirror. It was all fine. More than fine. She'd decided against her usual academic clothes, and went with her instinct, wearing a traditional abaya. It felt right, and the more Zavian went against feeling, the more she was for it.

She also knew that any nerves would vanish the moment she began talking about her work, the moment the passion she felt for it kicked in and overcame any superficial nerves. People wanted passion these days in their news and entertainment—everyone, that is, except Zavian. And yet he was one of the most passionate men she knew, deep down. And one with the most self-control and self-discipline. For a few long moments she imagined what that passion might be like for him, for her, and for his country, if he let the control and discipline slip. She'd seen glimpses of it and knew it was a life-giving and life-changing moment when he allowed it to show. It was for her, and it would be for his people, if only they were allowed to see the real man.

But that wasn't real life. Real life was where people— where Zavian—refused to acknowledge such feelings and instead dealt with the real. And so could she. For now, at least.

She picked up the things she needed and walked out of the office and down to the exhibition room. This was her real life, she reminded herself—museum rooms, TV cameras and the dusty objects she lived her life through. Bringing the past to the present. All she had to do was what Zavian did with ease—stop feeling.

THERE WOULD BE no future for them, Zavian repeated to himself for the millionth time. She demanded love, and he didn't do love. End of story. Or it would have been if he could stop seeing her, stop hearing about her, stop thinking about her.

Because despite being king, Zavian's wish to avoid

Gabrielle had proved elusive. Sure, he may have managed to not spend any time with her—something she obviously felt equally strongly about—but if he'd wished to avoid the sight of her, and talk about her, he'd been disappointed.

Every job she did was excellent, according to the museum director, who sung her praises at every opportunity. He couldn't get through a meeting without someone bringing up her name and commending her on her work and her vision for the country and its artifacts.

All he heard was how wonderful she was—a fact he couldn't deny—and there had even been veiled suggestions about her suitability for him. People knew they were friends, but few people knew just how close they were. Although, since the celebration of poetry in the desert, word had begun to get around. Something he regretted.

And this afternoon appeared to be no different. He'd intended to watch the new video released for the celebrations—something to bring his mind to focus on the important events coming up. Instead, all he saw was a close-up of Gabrielle explaining her work with that passion, which landed a punch straight into his gut.

He was pushed down on the chair by the force of the blow. She'd forgotten herself. He could see that. Her eyes were with her work, the history, her life. There was something incredibly seductive about seeing someone unaware or conscious of themselves, living only through their emotions and thoughts, both one.

The desert wind had blown her blonde hair free of her hijab, and it was like pale satin under the hot sun. Her face had become tanned since she'd returned to Gharb Havilah, making her blue eyes even bluer. He remembered them open, startled, as she climaxed in his arms. And in that moment he knew that he was not only fooling himself, but his vizier, and the whole country.

He slumped in his chair, put his head in his hands and acknowledged the visceral response he had for her wasn't confined to his body. She was more than a body he craved, more than a mind he respected, she was... herself. A woman who his heart beat for, a woman he could no more be without than the air that he breathed. He looked up, startled. Was that love? Could it be that, without any effort or desire from him, she'd shattered the defenses he'd built around his heart so effectively he hadn't even seen them fall?

He couldn't have said how long he continued to sit there. But the sunlight tracked across the room, his phone rang without answering, his vizier came and went—somehow understanding his need to be alone for once—and made sure he was given the space. Space to think about how he could convey to the woman he loved, that he did, indeed, love her. And that it was no mere words, no mere ticking a box, nothing that he was saying to keep her. But that his love was real. How could he show her that, after all he'd said and done?

It wasn't until the daylight had faded completely from the sky that the answer came into his mind and stuck there. He knew what he had to do, even if he didn't much like it.

CHAPTER 11

*G*abrielle scanned the headlines, flicked across to another site, and felt her nausea increase. It seemed everywhere on the internet guesses were being made as to who the King of Gharb Havilah would marry. Rumors were flying back and forth, trying to predict the king's forthcoming announcement. And there was no shortage of suggestions as to the identity of the woman. None of them, she noticed, included her.

Were they guessing, or did they know something she didn't? And what would it matter anyway? She'd be gone in a few days, back to England, returning to her academic life far away from the heat and dust of the desert, thousands of miles from where her heart lay.

She closed her computer too firmly. Some of her colleagues glanced across at her, as the sound echoed around the museum. She scraped back her chair and walked over to them as they waited to join the formal opening of the bi-millennial celebrations, which signaled the end of her work here, in Gharb Havilah.

As she responded to her colleagues, contributing to the

conversation, she marveled at how normal she sounded. She'd learned well from Zavian, because she'd managed to do the impossible and had frozen her feelings, leaving them solid and compact, encased in lead. She couldn't allow herself to examine the feelings, reflect on them in any way. That, she knew, would come later. Much later, when she was safely away from this place, away from Zavian. Until that time, she had no choice but to ignore the feelings which weighed heavily inside her. She had the next two days to get through first.

She smoothed down the deep red satin gown that she'd borrowed for the gala evening. The museum director's wife had extravagant tastes in clothes, and had insisted on lending Gabrielle the dress once she'd seen it on her. Gabrielle would have preferred something quieter, something more subtle, but the director's wife had refused to allow Gabrielle to try on any of her other dresses after she'd seen Gabrielle in that one.

"It would be a crime, my dear," she'd whispered conspiratorially in Gabrielle's ear. "It's your last night, and after all you've done for the museum, the celebrations, and the country, it's time you took your share of the limelight." The woman had stepped back with a smile and eyed her as she lit her cigarette. "And allow some people to see you for who you really are."

In the end, Gabrielle hadn't any choice. She had nothing else suitable for the gala opening. Besides, she didn't want to upset the woman. There weren't many people who'd shown interest in who Gabrielle was outside of her professional roles.

She paused in front of a mirror and automatically reached up to touch her hair, unrecognizable in the sleek french bun which her friend had insisted the hairdresser arrange for her. And the makeup... She blinked at her reflection and, reassuringly it blinked back, otherwise she might not have believed this Audrey Hepburn like image reflected back at her.

She walked away quickly. What did it matter if she looked like herself or someone else? A few days and she'd be out of here.

～

ZAVIAN HAD CHOSEN the gala evening before the bi-millennial celebrations officially got underway to face Gabrielle. He'd do what he had to do—and quickly—at the beginning of the evening, and then there'd be enough time to finalize the following day's timetable, including their betrothal.

Easy, he thought as he fidgeted with his tie in the mirror. As he went over what he was going to do, it seemed simple. Several boxes had already been ticked, bullet points achieved. All he'd done was add one to the list. The love one. He'd approach that as he had the others. Tell her that he'd been mistaken, that there appeared to be more to his feelings than he'd initially thought, feelings he assumed to be love. And, if they were, then he did indeed, love her.

He smiled at himself in the mirror. It was simply a matter of perspective. Just because he apparently loved her, it didn't mean to say he had to veer to the emotionally unstable depths of others. He could encompass this love thing into his view of himself. With a bit of effort, anyway.

It would be fine; he nodded reassuringly to himself. He'd simply stick to his plan, explain to her that all was well in the love department, and she would agree to marry him. The rest would be history, and his future.

He paused as his eyes rose to see his own, not so certain ones, in his reflection. Ridiculous to question himself! All would go according to plan. He refused to believe it wouldn't. He turned away abruptly and met Naseer's gaze. He'd confided his plans to his vizier who'd agreed with them.

"It will all go according to plan, Your Majesty. There is nothing to fear."

"Of course not. I do not fear..." He hesitated. "Anything," he said quietly, not quite believing his own statement, because he had the sneaking suspicion that he was almost a little afraid of one person. Minds and bodies he could control. But hearts? They were proving to be very different beasts.

He strode into the ballroom and looked around. It was full already. Music failed to cover the excited chatter of people dressed to the nines. Tonight was all about coming together and had no formal component. That would happen on the next day. He scanned the room once more but failed to see her. A dark gloom fell upon his spirits as Naseer introduced him to a visiting dignitary.

He uttered pleasantries, hardly aware of what he was saying, as his thoughts raced in an entirely different direction. Had she returned home before the celebrations began? No. She wouldn't have risked her college's financial situation. Besides, he would have been told. In that case, she'd remained in her room, stubbornly refusing to attend something he'd specifically asked her to attend. The idea that firstly, she refused to agree to his request, and secondly that his plans would be potentially thwarted, sparked a fire of anger inside.

He'd go and find her, wherever she was, and tell her what he needed to say to her. It was all he could think about now. He was beginning not to care how he told her, his rehearsed words could go out the window, just so long as he released the burden of his words and told her. It was a fact, that was all—a fact she needed to know.

He turned to Naseer, ignoring the upturned faces of the

others, obviously awaiting some response from him. "I have to go, Naseer, I—"

His words were interrupted as his eye caught a flash of red not far from him. The woman had her back to him. The red dress fell from her shoulders, exposing the creamy skin of her back, underlining it with a scoop of cowl-shaped red silk, curved just above her behind.

There was nothing in the clothes or the hair which he recognized but something in her air, the way she held herself. Then she half-turned, and he caught sight of the line of her jaw and knew it was her.

Leaving the baffled group behind for his vizier to deal with, Zavian walked directly to her. People fell away as he made a direct line for her. She turned, and suddenly he was before her. Other people in her group shuffled, muttered and, after the odd comment, stepped away slightly.

She curtseyed. "Your Majesty," she said.

"I wish to speak to you, Gabrielle."

She inclined her head. "Of course, Your Majesty."

"Drop that. It's just us."

She looked around. "Just us surrounded by hundreds of people."

"Ignore them. They do not exist for me."

Her lips quirked into a brief smile. "I love the way you can ignore anything you don't wish to see."

"Do you?"

She shook her head. "Actually, no, I don't."

It was his turn to feel a fleeting smile drift to his lips. "And I love the way you change your mind. Frequently."

"When I said, 'I love the way you can ignore anything', I meant I can't *believe* the way you ignore things."

"Ah, so when you use the word 'love' I shouldn't believe it."

She looked around but didn't answer.

"Gabrielle?"

She turned to him. "Yes?"

"I asked you a question."

"I thought it was a statement. Language is so difficult," she continued. "Always open to interpretation. Words are easy to say, it's the people you have to believe in, not the words. Anyway…"

She looked away as if searching to escape and turned to walk away. He wasn't about to let that happen. It was now or never. He had to get that box ticked so he could proceed with his plans.

"Well, I hope you believe me when I tell you I love you."

Even to his ears, the words didn't sound convincing— nothing like the films. Convincing or not, Gabrielle stopped in her tracks. She turned her head to look at him, brow knitted, her mouth open. "What?" The word sounded strangely strangled.

He cleared his throat. "I love you." Again, it didn't sound like he'd imagined it would. He, who rarely was aware of people, was now conscious of looks being shot his way. He wanted this wound up. He shifted onto his other leg. "So… what do you think?" He winced inside of himself—he never sounded needy, but it appeared he was now.

She turned to face him. It was she who appeared unaware now of onlookers. "What do I think? I think you're saying words that you believe I'd like to hear. That's what I think."

He sighed with impatience as he heard his name called by his vizier. He turned to see him approaching along with King Amir and King Roshan. His time was running out. He turned back to Gabrielle and stepped closer to her so that only she could hear now.

"I'm saying what I feel."

"Really? It doesn't sound like that's what you feel."

"I don't know what I'm meant to sound like, but take it

from me, that's what I feel. All right?"

"All right?" she repeated back to him. Or was she repeating it? Perhaps she was confirming that everything was, indeed, all right.

"Isn't it?" he asked.

"Isn't it what?"

"All right? The fact that I love you. I assume you still love me, so that sorts everything."

She drew in a deep sigh. "You're incredible."

He narrowed his eyes. "The way you said that it doesn't sound like a good thing." He held up his hand to stop his vizier's impatient voice.

"Zavian!" she said, shaking her head.

"Your Majesty," butted in the vizier. "People are waiting to see you."

"Right," he said. "Right," he said to Gabrielle. "I have to go. But I want you to know that I've done what you said. I've considered the matter and concluded that you're right. I love you."

"There you go again."

"I'm repeating," he said clearly, "because you aren't responding to me as I anticipated."

She glanced at the vizier, who was giving her a black look. "You should go. You're expected elsewhere."

He drew her closer. "I'm not going anywhere until you tell me you understand. I love you. Three words you wanted, and I've given them to you. I assume that they're not unwelcome." He raised an imperious eyebrow. He couldn't seem to stop himself.

"Go, Zavian. We can talk about this later."

"No. I need to know now whether what I've said is sufficient for you to marry me."

She shook her head but smiled at the same time. True, it was a hard-to-read kind of a smile, but Zavian instinctively read it as a reassuring smile. He'd given her what she wanted. He relaxed his grip on her hand with relief.

"Good," he said. "I must go now. But there is nothing now to fear, Gabrielle. All will be well."

He raised a hand in greeting to the two kings who stood with amused smiles by the entrance, awaiting him. There was nothing to fear, he repeated to himself as he walked away from her, remembering her small smile. She'd said that words were of no importance on their own, and that you had to trust the person themselves. She trusted him. Of that, he was certain. Therefore all would be well. His plan could continue.

As GABRIELLE WATCHED Zavian greet the two kings who made up the ancient kingdom of Havilah, she shook her head, bemused and frustrated. How could he believe that him telling her he loved her like that changed anything? She knew what he'd done. He'd added the "love thing" to his bullet point list and now considered it had been ticked. Well, he needed to do a whole lot more than tell her. He needed to *show* her he loved her because until he did, she wouldn't believe that he'd allowed the walls around his heart to fall, wouldn't believe that they could have a life together.

She wished she could disappear into the night, into the shadows of her suite of rooms. But she had her duties to perform that night. Just one evening and the next few days and then she could leave, away from the temptations and jeering reminders of a life that might have been hers.

SHEIKH AMIR LOOKED at Zavian thoughtfully. "What's going on, Zavian? I haven't seen you this jumpy since we were teenagers, and you had your eye on that girl."

Amir's comment broke Zavian's train of thought, and he glanced around to see that both Amir and Roshan were watching him with barely concealed amusement.

"You're right, Amir," said Roshan, leaning back in his chair and taking a quick sip of his drink, "Zavian is plotting something." He cocked his head to one side with a considering air. "Plotting something that he's not quite sure about. Hm. Interesting." He looked at Amir. "Since when has our friend ever been not quite sure about something?"

"There's only one thing that he's unsure of, and that's about matters of the heart."

"Ah, yes," replied Roshan. "Now he really should come to me on that score. I happen to be an expert in matters of the heart."

Zavian scowled at them both. "I need no help."

"Of course," Roshan leaned forward, rubbing his fists against his lips consideringly. "You are an expert. You have such a successful track record."

"And you have, I suppose. All you have left behind you is a string of broken hearts."

"But not mine. That, I would suggest, is being successful."

Zavian shook his head. Roshan was incorrigible, and hell would freeze over before he took any advice from him. In the relationship department, anyway.

He looked around the room with satisfaction. Everything was going according to plan. *His* plan. He caught Gabrielle's eye as she listened to the foreign ambassador who was keen on promoting cultural and tourist links between their countries, and smiled at her. She smiled back, their eyes caught in an intimate moment, which transcended the room. It calmed any outstanding fears from his earlier conversation.

It was time. He rose, and she sat back, puzzled, as silence fell in the room. As he started to speak, all eyes fell upon him just as he'd planned. This would be the perfect opening to the celebrations, the icing on the cake. It would place his country at the forefront of the world's media as they gloried in Gharb Havilah's past, in its prosperous present and its promising future. So much had changed over the past few generations, but he was here now at a point where they could move forward with confidence. After a short, formal speech in which he welcomed guests and spoke of the meaning the celebration had to his country, he moved on to the part of his speech about which none of his advisors had been told. He didn't meet his vizier's direct look, but he could feel it as he continued.

"I'd like to end now where I began. The importance of Gharb Havilah's future is dependent on the people who live here, and a leadership committed to its people and culture... a leader who is committed to family life." He turned to Gabrielle. "And what better time to thank Dr. Gabrielle Taylor for her commitment to our culture and her work on the celebrations. Gabrielle has made the study of Gharb Havilah's past her life's work. She's been an inspiration to us all, and most particularly to me. She sums up what makes Gharb Havilah great. A love of the people and the country. And it gives me great pleasure to announce our engagement."

There was a moment of stunned silence. Royalty rarely provided the unexpected, but then there was a burst of applause and cheers as various leaders rose and clapped, turning first to the king and then to Gabrielle.

Zavian smiled back, acknowledging the cheers and good wishes. Ever since that moment in the desert, he'd known the match would meet the approval of his people. And it seems he was correct. Even a glance at his vizier reassured him. From initial disbelief, his vizier was nodding slowly and joining in with the general sense of celebration. The formality of the dinner dissolved, and people crowded around. Not least his two friends, Amir and Roshan.

There was only one person he couldn't see. There were people milling around between them.

Roshan clapped Zavian on the back. "You dark horse!" He grinned widely. "Seems like you know a bit more than you're letting on."

But Zavian wasn't in the mood to talk. He was trying to spot Gabrielle in the crowd.

"Where is she?"

The two other kings looked around. "There's some commotion moving over there. I think she's... yes, she's making her way to the exit."

They both looked at Zavian, who frowned. This wasn't his plan—nowhere near his plan.

"Maybe I was premature in my congratulations," said Roshan. "We'll cover for you, but I think you'd better go and track down your bride-to-be because it looks like she's just left the room."

He didn't waste any time following Roshan's advice. He moved swiftly through the crowds, which parted before him, but she must have run after she'd left the room because there was no sign of her.

He hesitated for a moment and considered where she might go to in the heat of the moment. It came to him in a flash. The gardens. He strode down the empty colonnaded walks, past the public areas of the palace, toward the older wing where the old, overgrown garden was. He saw her instantly, her red dress flashing against the dark greens of the palms and plants as she made her way to the privacy of the central fountain.

He followed her and watched for a few moments as she slumped down beside the fountain and put her head in her hands. That made him start forward.

"Gabrielle, tell me, what's the matter?"

She turned to him with a start, and he was surprised to

see not the emotion he'd expected on her face. She was furious.

"What's the matter?" She took his hand and flung it from her, folding her arms across her chest. He'd never seen her so angry before. "You've publicly humiliated me, and you ask me what the matter is?"

Anger sparked in him. "Humiliated? How is asking you to marry me a humiliation?"

"You. Didn't. Ask. Me!" Each word was spoken with vehemence.

"I hardly thought I needed to. I thought you'd made your feelings clear." For the first time, a shadow of doubt entered his mind. He couldn't have got it so wrong, surely?

She shook her head, her eyes bright, her mouth a firm line, a million miles from the kiss he'd imagined giving her at this moment. "Whatever I said, whatever I feel for you, it's totally overshadowed by behavior such as this!"

"Me asking you to marry you is bad behavior?"

"I repeat," she said in a dangerously low tone. "You *didn't* ask me. Do you really imagine that the public announcement of our engagement would result in marriage?"

"Yes." It was the only answer he could think of. Because he hadn't, in a million years, imagined any other outcome.

"And just in that answer I know that we could never marry."

"What are you talking about?" He was getting angry now. "We talked about the future, you said you needed to know I loved you, and I told you I did. What's the problem?"

She clamped her hand to her chest, where her heart rested beneath. "The problem is that I don't believe you love me. All I know is that you said the words to me."

"But you trust my word, surely?"

Her hesitation said it all. "I know that you believe what

you say, but, Zavian, I'm not sure that your definition of love is the same as mine. I can't believe in it."

"Then what, Gabrielle, do I have to do to make you believe that I love you."

"You have to do more than tell me like it's something you've signed off on. You have to show me that you have feelings for me."

"You *know* I have feelings for you."

The folded her arms defensively across her chest. "I know you want me in your bed."

He raked his fingers through his hair and twisted away. "It's more than that."

"It's not what I'm seeing."

He flung his arms open, full of anger and frustration. He was floored. "Words? You want words?"

"Yes. I want more than a box ticked. I want more than the word regurgitated and spat back at me as if I were a chick needing it to survive." She shook her head. "But that small morsel isn't enough to move forward on, isn't enough to believe in, isn't enough to sustain our relationship with."

He suddenly realized. "You don't believe me. You think I'm lying."

"No, there you're wrong. I think you believe in what you're saying, but to me, they are words without emotion. It's not in the words."

"Then what is it?"

"It's in what lies behind them. It's in your manner, in your heart, showing through your words."

He withdrew his hand from her and placed his hands on his hips. "So now I have to work out how to get my heart to show through? You ask too much, Gabrielle. Too much." With that, he turned and stalked away. Too quickly to hear her reply.

"I ask too little."

CHAPTER 12

*H*is vizier was waiting for Zavian's return.

"Where are you going?" asked Naseer. Zavian stopped in his tracks and shook his head.

"Back to the reception, of course."

"There's no of course about it," said Naseer in a tone most unlike his usual respectful one. "You and I need to talk."

"Naseer!" Zavian said. "The last thing I wish to do now is to talk to you."

"Zavian!" said Naseer, using the same tone. "This is something I should have done years ago. And would have, if I'd listened to the girl's grandfather, rather than your father! Now, come with me."

"But—"

"The rest can wait, this can't."

Naseer's tone chastened Zavian. "What's happened?"

Naseer's mouth was a firm line as he shot him a dark look before proceeding toward a stateroom. Zavian entered, and Naseer closed the door firmly behind them. The place was in shadow and private.

Neither made to sit down. Naseer turned and crossed his

arms, his back to the door. "Your father was a tough man, Zavian, and he was especially tough on you."

Zavian shrugged. "It's of no importance now."

"Yes, it is. It made you the man you are today. Also tough, strong and determined, but you lost something you had in abundance as a boy. You lost your ability to be affectionate, you stopped showing your love, and eventually, you stopped feeling that love. Any emotion you had became twisted into something else. Power, lust..." Naseer shook his hand, indicating a range of other things. And then he pointed to where the feast had just taken place. "And that, in there, shows your ineptness." He shook his head. "I've been remiss. I thought..."

"What did you think?" Any clue, Zavian would gratefully have received.

"I thought your father was right. At one time, anyway. I thought that maybe the soft heart you had in your youth was a weakness, a hindrance." He pursed his lips with regret. "But it was only later that I realized it wasn't because your father considered your affection weak that he wanted to eradicate it, but because he was jealous and scared." He looked Zavian directly in the eye. "It was he who was the weak man. And it was his weakness which was the end of him. You have a capacity for greatness, which your father never had." He stepped closer to Zavian, closer than was ever usual between a king and his subject. "Find your heart again, Zavian. For only that will connect you with your people. For only that will connect you with the woman who I know, deep down, you love." He nodded, and stepped away. "That is all I have to say. Go now and think about what I have said. Your announcement has been well received, if not with a little puzzlement at its suddenness. Everyone, excepting your cabinet and ministers, was expecting an announcement of betrothal between you and the Tawazun sheikha."

"That will now fall to Roshan."

"Yes, and he had better not fail us. But that is up to him and his advisers to pursue. For us, all is dependent on you persuading Gabrielle that you truly do want to wed her. She loves you, anyone can see that. But also anyone can see that she is an extraordinary woman who needs security from her husband, which she has never experienced in the rest of her life. And the only thing she can trust is the one thing you need to find again in your heart." The vizier tapped Zavian on his chest as he said the final words, in a gesture far too familiar for one of his advisers, but reminiscent of their relationship when Zavian was young.

As Zavian watched Naseer walk away and return to the reception to ensure that any rough water was smoothed over, Zavian realized he'd just been given a reprimand and told to sort himself out. For a moment, he wavered as to whether to be angry with his vizier but the moment passed, and he smiled to himself. Because he knew, deep down, that Naseer was correct.

ZAVIAN RETURNED to the sanctity of his suite of rooms and paced the floor. He felt as if he'd been run over by a truck. He stopped by the window and looked, unseeing, into the night. No, not a truck, but by a force of a woman who'd been deprived of security and love her whole life, and a woman who was also strong enough to hold out for what she wanted.

He rubbed his chest, where a deep ache lay. Between Gabrielle and his vizier, he felt as if his heart had been cracked open like a walnut shell, revealing a tender, shy, vulnerable center. His love ran deep, body deep, soul deep. The only question was, how could he convince her, given every other heartless thing he'd done in his life, done to her, that he loved her—truly and forever?

He stopped pacing at his desk and glanced down. Her name swam into view. The monograph she'd written on the Khasham Qur'an. Dr. Gabrielle Taylor. He flicked it open. Words, full of words. Words carefully placed together to create a whole, a truth, which no one could now dispute. Before her monograph, there had been uncertainty around the origins, but the words had confirmed everything. Without the words, all was uncertainty, but now with them, there was a single truth which no one could challenge. No one.

He closed her book and sat down and put his head in his hands. His head throbbed with the painful knowledge that he'd got so much, so wrong. With his love of black and white, he'd baldly said the words to her, informed her that he loved her. But it wasn't enough to convey the meaning. For that he needed subtlety and passion. For that... his eyes strayed to the book of poetry... he needed poetry.

It was early in the morning the next day when he strode through the palace to Gabrielle's rooms. After a sleepless night, he could wait no longer. He knocked on the door, but there was no answer. He hesitated, pulled out his phone and rang. But again there was no answer and it wasn't ringing inside the room. He knocked again. Tentatively he opened the door, but all hesitation left him at what he saw there. The room was empty, clear of her things. He strode in, wanting to see if anything had been left behind. But there was nothing.

He called the housekeeping people. They'd tidied her room, as she'd requested before she left.

Left where? No one knew.

"Then find out!" He slammed down the phone. Zavian stormed onto the terrace, gripped the wall, and looked around his city as if hoping to find her. The heat was intense, both inside of him and outside now. He needed air, he needed to breathe. But most of all, he needed her.

His phone rang, and he answered it immediately. He rang off as soon as he heard the information he needed. Her cell phone had been traced to a location in the desert. As he slipped his phone back into his pocket, his mind went over the options. No, there was only one place she'd gone to. And it wasn't the border as others had suggested. It was somewhere much more meaningful than that. It was somewhere he'd stopped her going to when she'd first arrived. She was returning to the one place where she'd ever been certain of being loved.

GABRIELLE CRUNCHED the Landrover into gear and headed north, into the desert. It was where she wanted to be, and she was sure that it was where no one would think to look, least of all Zavian.

It was night before she reached it. The old house was deserted now, and the nearby village was quiet. There was a crescent moon perched above the horizon, and stars were beginning to emerge. She drove up to the high walls and unlocked the gates. The keys had always been on her keyring. For the past year, they'd been a mere reminder of a past life, but now they were useful again. She parked the Landrover in front of the stables, now empty of their white Arab horses. The hinges on the wooden doors had come loose, the doors hanging.

She got out of the vehicle and left her bags at the front door. She'd let herself into her old family home later. But now she'd explore, for the last time, the place where her grandfather had raised her, and taught her the importance of love.

She pushed open the gate to the walled courtyard and was immediately taken back in time. Here, sheltered from the fierce winds of the desert, and fed by the underground streams, the plants, shrubs and trees still flourished. A swift flew overhead, catching the last insects in the rapidly fading twilight. The scent of the flowers and shrubs was overpowering after the dryness of the desert.

She walked down the path, which led to the center of the gardens. She trailed her fingers along the leaves, sticky with nectar, and looked up into the towering trees, untouched by a gardener's hands for years. Then she heard it, a songbird and the trickle of water.

She followed the sound to the central fountain. A small bird has tilted his beak back and was singing loudly in the silence of the desert.

"Just you and me, birdie," she said, taking a seat on the bench. The bird continued to sing, somehow tame, not frightened by this stranger in the midst of its loneliness.

She couldn't have said how long she sat listening to the bird but was suddenly aware that it had stopped, and was no longer on the fountain. And that darkness had fallen. A stray beam of moonlight filtered through the leaves, casting shimmering shadows over the water. It was only then that the tears came.

She stayed sitting without moving, as the tears streamed down her face from deep inside of her. She'd kept them in too long, she knew. Ever since that day, twelve months before, when she'd realized she had to leave Zavian. And had realized with equal certainty that she loved him.

She'd done her best to do the right thing, just as her grandfather had always told her she should. And she'd trust nothing less than love, just as her grandfather had told her. He'd loved her grandmother for every minute of her short life, just as her parents had loved each other. Her grandfather had shown her that there was nothing more important than love in everything he did, everything he'd said.

So, she'd walked away from Zavian, and made sure he couldn't follow. She'd been outwitted then, but she'd make sure she wasn't outwitted now because she refused to compromise on this one point. She knew what happened to couples without love. Zavian's parents were examples of that.

She'd thought he'd brought her here to punish her for leaving him, by rekindling their passion only for him to discard her. Given how angry he'd been, retribution was the only thing she could imagine. After all, it was something his father had been expert at.

And maybe he had at first, but now he wanted her back. But how could she stay when he didn't love her? If the walls around his heart were so strong that they refused to feel, what if circumstances dictated she should no longer be with him? What if people turned against her and wanted her gone? Without love, she was disposable. And she refused to be that. She was worth more than that. Her parents' and grandparents' love for each other had shown her that, and her grandfather's constant love and advice had driven the point home.

She suddenly felt incredibly tired. Drained. Exhausted. All she wanted was to curl up and stop thinking, stop feeling. She took a deep breath of the scented, familiar air—air that had surrounded her growing up—and let it infiltrate her body, sending a soothing calm to her frayed nerves. She succumbed to temptation and lay down. Within seconds she was asleep.

ZAVIAN CLUNKED his door shut firmly, and looked up at the house where he'd fallen in love with Gabrielle. Of course, then, he hadn't admitted it. It was only now that he could, and he saw it through different eyes. The building's traditional facade, the smell of the dry desert air edged with perfumes coming from the abundant garden, took him back immediately to those days when they'd first discovered each other. The sights and sounds by-passed his mind—the place where he'd lived his life—and went straight to the place he'd spent his whole life denying, until now—his heart.

He rubbed his chest with the heel of his hand to try to rid it of the ache, which was growing as he realized he might have missed Gabrielle and lost her. Time was running out. He looked with increasing desperation around the building. No lights were on. For a moment, Zavian wondered if he'd been correct about her destination. Then he shone the light from his phone around the courtyard, and it caught the gleam of a vehicle parked in front of the stables. He went over to it. It was hers all right. But where was she? He gave the stables a cursory look, but there was no sign of her there, nor in the vehicle. And there were no lights on in the house.

Then he heard it—the sound of a nocturnal bird in the gardens. He huffed a relieved sigh. Of course. She'd always loved those gardens. He pushed open the gate and walked around the perimeter of the gardens, checking each arbor carefully before moving on. The outside path wound in like a snail's shell, moving ever closer to its central feature—the fountain.

He stopped as soon as he saw her. She was curled up along the bench, her head propped on her arm, facing the fountain as if she'd found peace there before her eyes had fluttered closed. Under the moonlight, he could see her features were relaxed, but there was a glistening smudge beneath her eyes, and her abaya against which her cheek pressed was dark with tears.

His immediate urge was to go to her, to pull her into his arms and hold her until the hurt went away. But he now knew, because of her, that he couldn't erase the pain. It was beyond his ability to control people, to change people, to make the pain go away, or to bring happiness. All he could do was be here for her, to try to help her if she wanted help, and ask her to stay. And to do that, he had to control himself, not anyone else. He drew in a deep breath and flexed his hands and stepped forward.

THE SPLASH of water had lulled her to sleep, and that same sense of peace filled her as she awoke. Gabrielle didn't open her eyes immediately. The voice in her head was as calming as the water which flowed from the broken fountain across the once magnificent paved areas to the lush garden. Then she heard it again—her name. And it wasn't in her dreams any longer.

She opened her eyes with a start as she tried to figure out where she was, and more importantly, who she was with.

The moon was higher now and, together with the stars, they gifted the landscape—the leaves, the water, the stone—with a silver mystery.

"Gabrielle?" His voice was soft but unmistakable.

She jumped up with a cry. "Zavian! What are you doing here?"

He didn't move, simply sat there, looking up at her, making no move to come to her. She pressed her hand against her heart. "You startled me. I thought I was alone."

"I'm sorry to surprise you, but you know we couldn't leave it like that."

She stepped away from him, not knowing what he was here for, unsure of what was to come. "You're wrong. We *have* to leave it like that."

He reached out for her hand, and she couldn't do

anything but accept it. He slid his fingers through hers and gripped it like a lifeline.

"I'm so sorry for everything that has happened."

"You've come here to apologize?"

"Amongst other things, yes. I tried to buy you, Gabrielle." He shook his head. "Even as I say those words, it sounds crazy. I can hardly believe that is what I did."

"Crazy is an understatement."

"And I know you're angry with me, rightly so. But I'm a different person now. You've made me that different person."

"Not too different, I hope," she said, with a faint smile.

"I love you, Gabrielle. And I cannot live without you."

Her eyes filled with tears to hear the words she'd waited so long to hear, to believe the prayer he'd offered her. Her mind stilled, and her speech froze. The silence between them was broken only by the rustle of leaves that had grown above the protection of the wall, and the murmur of the water as it flowed across the weed-clogged rills.

"Gabrielle..." His words sounded as if they'd been wrenched from him. "Speak to me."

She gasped in a breath, refusing to believe his words. She had to take them at face value. She couldn't risk doing anything else. "You're just saying the words you know I want to hear."

He shook his head. "No. Not anymore. Gabrielle, I can't speak without feeling now."

He licked his lips, and then he started to speak, and Gabrielle could hardly believe her ears.

"Between what is said and not meant
And what is meant and not said
Most of love is lost."

This was no punchy, bullet-pointed sentence, no instruction, no adamant statement. This was poetry. After he'd

163

finished speaking, she shook her head, hardly daring to believe her ears.

"'Most of Love is Lost' by Gibran Khalil Gibran," murmured Gabrielle.

Zavian nodded. "It seemed apt." He shrugged. "I have failed, Gabrielle, to persuade you that I love you. Every time I tried, I seemed to send you further from me. I am no good with words and like the poet says, I see my love disappearing like smoke into the air, lost between words said, and words not said." He opened his arms in a gesture of surrender. "That's it. I have no more words to say or leave unsaid. It's up to you to believe in my love, or else it is lost. Do you trust my love is real? That is what it comes down to."

Gabrielle's frown deepened, and she glanced at him, unsure now, and edgy. She nodded, too rapidly, as if trying to understand something. But still, she didn't speak.

He smiled. "It seems you are at a loss for words, so I must continue. Without you, my life is a half-life, a life lived behind a heavy curtain, looking out at the world, but not hearing it, not feeling it, not participating in it. You've shown me that life cannot be lived by calculation alone. It needs heart. And you have mine." He brought their joined hands to his lips and kissed the back of her hand. "So, you see, I cannot do without you. Because if you go, you will take my heart, and I cannot survive."

She half-laughed, half-sobbed.

"Marry me, Gabrielle. Please, marry me. Together we can deal with whatever comes our way. We're stronger together. We're right together. We're meant to be together. I feel it profoundly, deeply, here inside. Please, marry me. Will you share my life with me, will you love me, and will you bear my children, will you allow me to care for you, adore you, cherish you always, and to be obsessed by you, forever?"

"Forever is a long time," she said with a smile.

"Too long without you. Not long enough with you."

She grinned and shook her head.

"Marry me, Gabrielle."

She nodded. "Yes."

It was the only word that could emerge before his lips claimed hers for a kiss, which felt like it would go on for a thousand years... or two.

EPILOGUE

Zavian stood with his two friends—Amir and Roshan—watching his wedding reception come to a close. Thanks to Gabrielle and her new best friend, Ruby, Amir's wife, the usually austere reception room had been transformed into party central, complete with lights, dance floor and balloons, courtesy of Ruby and Amir's son, Hani.

Now, at the end of the day, some of the balloons had drifted to the marble floor. He noticed Naseer clicking his fingers for someone to take them away. He smiled to himself. No matter how fond Naseer had become of Gabrielle, he doubted Naseer would ever get used to informality in the palace.

"You certainly didn't waste any time," said Roshan, taking a sip of his champagne. He indicated Zavian's advisor, Naseer. "I bet the old man wasn't impressed with only having a month to organize the wedding."

Zavian smiled as he remembered Naseer's reaction. "Indeed. But he didn't make a fuss. I think he was relieved I was getting married at all."

"That anyone would have you," added Amir, with a smile.

Zavian's gaze rested on Gabrielle, who was talking with Ruby and Hani. "She nearly didn't," he commented.

"No," said Roshan. "She's far too clever to consider a wealthy, powerful king to be a good match."

Zavian ignored Roshan's comment. Zavian knew that, despite how sarcastic it sounded, Roshan meant it. For all his outward appearance of confidence, there was something very unconfident that sat at the heart of Roshan. Sometimes Zavian wasn't even sure if Roshan liked himself. But he was too focused on Gabrielle to question Roshan further.

"You're right. It had to be love," said Zavian. "And, as it happened. I'm madly in love with her." The words of love came easily now.

Gabrielle glowed in the soft lights, outshining any of the other women in their dazzling dresses. At that moment, Gabrielle looked up and caught his gaze. She smiled, that wonderfully warm smile, that heated his gut, and lower. He sucked in a sharp breath as he imagined taking her to bed. Their lovemaking had always been intoxicating, but in the past few weeks, it had become even more intense. Gabrielle was more sensitive than ever to his touch.

Roshan groaned. "For goodness sake, take her to bed, now, and be done with it." He shook his head, and Amir laughed.

Amir clapped his hand on Roshan's back and addressed Zavian. "Our friend Roshan is a cynic, Zavian."

Reluctantly, Zavian withdrew his gaze from Gabrielle, who was making her way over to him with Ruby and Hani. "Yes, but not for long. The Tawazun princess is beautiful, and you've always appreciated a beautiful woman, Roshan. Maybe the appreciation will develop into love."

Roshan shrugged and glanced around the room as if searching for someone. Zavian frowned. There was something restless about Roshan tonight, which was different. He was usually the life and soul of the party. But, tonight, he appeared almost subdued. Zavian opened his mouth to ask Roshan what was going on when his thoughts were derailed by Gabrielle's touch on his arm. He pulled her into his arms and kissed her. He didn't care who witnessed it; he adored his new wife.

It was Gabrielle who pulled away first and exchanged a knowing look with Ruby.

"Come on, Amir, we must be leaving," said Ruby, looking like she'd just stepped out of a fashion shoot—stunning as ever. "It's way past Hani's bedtime."

Amir, Ruby and Hani said their goodbyes, and Zavian and Gabrielle watched them leave.

"Hani is a different boy now he's well," said Zavian.

"And now he's with his mom. Ruby is an amazing mother. She's expecting, you know."

"That's good. A brother or sister for Hani. Amir has always wanted a big family."

Gabrielle stepped in front of him and locked her fingers around the back of his neck, looking up at him with a secretive smile. "And do you?"

He'd almost forgotten what they were talking about.

"Do I what?"

"Want a big family?"

"Huge. I want many, many children, Gabrielle," he murmured as he kissed her. "In fact, I think we should leave now and continue to work on this particular objective. There's no time to waste."

She laughed, a delicious giggle which wrapped around the heart he'd spent so many years ignoring.

"As it happens, my love," she said, "it appears the first time was enough."

"Enough?" he whispered. He didn't dare to believe her meaning. "Gabrielle?"

She nodded, and her eyes swam with tears. But they weren't sad ones, her wide smile told him that much. She took his hand and placed it on her stomach, and for the first time, he realized the meaning of the slight thickening around her waist. Not, it appeared, the result of her increased appetite.

"I'm pregnant, Zavian. It must have been the night of the *khamseen*, in the cave."

If he'd ever been in any doubt as to the state of his heart, it was blown away by how he now felt. He'd thought he couldn't love her any more; he'd thought wrong.

"I love you, Gabrielle." He caressed her stomach, where his hand still lay.

She laughed. "I think I know, now, Zavian. You tell me often enough."

He kissed her forehead. "And I'm going to continue telling you"—he kissed her nose—"throughout every day of our long lives together." He lingered on the kiss on her lips. "Time for bed, my queen."

Hand in hand, they walked through the emptying reception room and out into the garden. As Zavian glanced across the garden, he halted. For a moment, he thought he'd seen Roshan, his tall figure briefly visible in a patch of moonlight. He wasn't alone. A woman's profile was also caught in the moonlight, but it wasn't anyone he recognized. He shrugged. Roshan was no doubt up to no good, as usual.

He just hoped that, whatever he was doing, and whoever he was doing it with, it wouldn't jeopardize the future of the three sheikhs of Havilah.

AFTERWORD

Thank you for reading *Bought by the Sheikh*. I hope you enjoyed it! Reviews are always welcome—they help me, and they help prospective readers to decide if they'd enjoy the book.

The Sheikhs of Havilah series is comprised of:

The Sheikh's Secret Baby
Bought by the Sheikh
The Sheikh's Forbidden Lover

My other sheikh series is Desert Kings.

Wanted: A Wife for the Sheikh
The Sheikh's Bargain Bride
The Sheikh's Lost Lover
Awakened by the Sheikh
Claimed by the Sheikh
Wanted: A Baby by the Sheikh

If you've read all of the above, why not try out one of my other books? There is the **Italian Romance** series which begins with *Perfect*. Then there are two series set in New Zealand—**The Mackenzies**, and **Lantern Bay**. Against a backdrop of beautiful New Zealand locations—deserted beaches, Wellington towers, snow-capped mountains—the Mackenzie and Connelly families fall in love. But expect some twists and turns!

You can check out all my books on the following pages. And, if you'd like to know when my next book is available, you can sign up for my new release e-mail list via my website— https://www.dianafraser.com.

Happy reading!

Diana

∾

THE SHEIKH'S FORBIDDEN LOVER

BOOK 3 OF SHEIKHS OF HAVILAH

Forced apart for the sake of peace!

A playboy sheikh determined to ignore his heart, a beautiful sheikha for whom duty comes first. And a one-night stand which leads to complications...

Buy Now!

ALSO BY DIANA FRASER

Desert Kings

Wanted: A Wife for the Sheikh
The Sheikh's Bargain Bride
The Sheikh's Lost Lover
Awakened by the Sheikh
Claimed by the Sheikh
Wanted: A Baby by the Sheikh

The Sheikhs of Havilah

The Sheikh's Secret Baby
Bought by the Sheikh
The Sheikh's Forbidden Lover

The Mackenzies

The Real Thing
The PA's Revenge
The Marriage Trap
The Cowboy's Craving
The Playboy's Redemption
The Lakehouse Café

Lantern Bay

Yours to Give
Yours to Treasure

Yours to Cherish

Made in the USA
Coppell, TX
12 April 2021

53568451R00098